D1519242

A HEAVEN OF OTHERS

Starcherone Books, Buffalo, NY

A HEAVEN OF OTHERS

Being the True Account of a Jewish Boy

Jonathan Schwarzstein of Tchernichovsky Street

Jerusalem

and his *Post-Mortem* Adventures in

& Reflections on

the Muslim Heaven

▼

▲

as Said to Me and Said through Me

by an Angel of the One True God

Revealed to Me at Night

as if in a Dream

Text copyright © 2007, 2010 Joshua Cohen
Images copyright © 2007, 2010 Michael Hafftka
Second Edition

ISBN13: 978-0-9788811-4-6
ISBN10: 0-9788811-4-1

Library of Congress Cataloging-in-Publication Data
    Cohen, Joshua, 1980-
    A heaven of others / Joshua Cohen.
    p. cm.
    ISBN 0-9788811-4-1 (alk. paper)
    1. Boys--Israel--Fiction. 2. Jews--Israel--Fiction.
    3. Victims of terrorism--Israel--Fiction. 4. Paradise
    (Islam)--Fiction. 5. Future life--Fiction. I. Title.
    PS3553.O42434H43 2008
    813'.54--dc22
    2007032241

Starcherone Books thanks Abraham and Julienne
Krasnoff for their generous support.

Printed in the United States of America
Starcherone Books
PO Box 303
Buffalo, NY 14201

To Alexander Fried,

of Czechoslovakia, Nazism, Sovietism, Austria, Belgium, Canada, Israel & the Czech Republic...

The last of the last Europeans.

נֶפֶשׁ הַיֶּלֶד הָרַךְ כְּבָר פָּסְקָה מִלְּחוֹם עַל עַצְמָהּ,
וְסָפְגָה וְקִבְּלָה הַכֹּל מִיַּד מַדְרִיכֶיהָ. וַתִּטַּפַּח
בְּקִרְבָּהּ תּוֹרַת הַזָּר, בִּרְבוֹת הַיָּמִים גַּם תֵּצֵא,
לְשִׂמְחַת הוֹרִים וּמוֹרִים, הַשַּׁעֲרָה - עֵגֶל מְלֻמָּד.
וְאוּלָם יֵשׁ שֶׁמֵּלַחַץ כְּבָלָיו יִשְׁתַּחֲרֵר הַיֶּלֶד,
וְנַפְשׁוֹ שִׂנְאָה מִסְתֶּרֶת, מַשְׂטֵמַת עוֹלָמִים נִמְלָאָה
לְכָל מַכְנִיעֶיהָ וְלַאֲשֶׁר אִנְּסוּהָ לְהַעֲרִיץ וּלְהַקְדִּישׁ
לַמְרוֹת רְצוֹנָהּ; וּבְאֵין מֶחָאָה אַחֶרֶת בְּיָדֶיהָ,
תִּדְבַּק בְּכָל אֲשֶׁר אִסּוּר מְעַנֶּיהָ חָל עָלָיו נַחֲרָמָיו.

שאול טשרניחובסקי, לביבות (אידיליה)

Sie stiessen zusammen auf der Strasse
Zwei Schicksale auf dieser Erde
Zwei Blutkreisläufe in ihrem Adernetz
Zwei Atmende auf ihrem Weg
in diesem Sonnensystem
Über ihre Gesichter zog eine Wolke fort
die Zeit hatte einen Sprung bekommen
Erinnern lugte herein
Ferne und Nähe waren Eines geworden
Von Vergangenheit und Zukunft
funkelten zwei Schicksale
und fielen auseinander —

Nelly Sachs, Glühende Rätsel: III

How did I get here, if I am still an I? If how and where is here? can still be asked and why?

He got here how he got here. How anyone gets here. How and where it is not my domain, this answering of questions. It is unbecoming. Truly, insulting. Beneath me. Below. Rather it is I, Who create these questions and endeavor to create them answerless. Unanswerable to anyone save the asker to whom — and do not fall into the wrong pit if it is in Me to ever create one — they are still unanswerable but who still must seek. To hide a find. To question my domain, my only power, rather the only power I allow myself in the how and in the here.

But rest assured that here was arrived at through no fault of his own. And that what is mine is my memory. A memory is all that is left and all that is mine — Which either begins or does it end only to begin all over again on what had been the most summery, swelteringly ripest pear day I can remember, I can the most.

I was with my parents but already without them, verily I was outside with the cars, amongst the birds and the beeswax I was old enough for alone. It was my birthday, my tenth, a toy birthday and so we were on the way to the toy store for my present but after And only after as the Queen always said this pilgrimage Had to be made.

A nail had been sticking through his shoe, killing it, shoe-through, my Aba's. In pain since yesterday's yesterday, ever since a nail had stuck through cow and foot, my Aba's.

Aba was in a shoe store with the Queen (that's how Ababa we often called him called Ima, Wife, Eve of my Lilith, Mommy, Mom, Hello Muddah, the Woman of the House or Apart-menthold, Bride), me I was, I was as bored as a baked good, the street an asphalt birthday cake rising the candle of me flickeringly impatient to reflect dimly in the window of the display under the sign saying SHOES, over the sign saying PERSONAL DATA SOLUTIONS reflected hazily inattentive in the window from a store of computers on the opposite side of the Blah blah blah. I was observing myself, my skin stretched across the rounding toes not yet scuffed of shoes not yet my size that never would be. Puffing myself out as if Hanukah

donuts were filling my cheeks, frying behind my eyes, I observed my I. Jelly limbs. What was reflected back to me was merely a reflection of my form — jam nose, mouth preserves — the shape of any not quite but almost ten-year-old, itchy in wait, twitchy with sun and the light and its heat and not the faces For examplish the Queen had once loved: the default Funny Face, the default Sad Face (opposites fulfill those as engaging as I once was), the Don't Disturb Me When I'm Watching TV Face, which I meant as much as the Keep the Beets Far Far Away From Me on the Other Opposite End of the Table Face, and which of what is me or isn't, I never wasn't. A toy, I just wanted a toy, to break to get another toy. To break next year or upon the New Year, which were never.

He stood there, beyond All. Alone despite any reflection, picking pants from tush. In hot Ennui Aba would say steeped in stirless Anomie and *vav kaf vav* A stupid day he'd say, Aba sitting to try on pair after pair, after pair, with the Queen standing-vetting, disapproving, mostly No-ing, anything but denying anyone but herself least of all. I remember I observed all this wonder through the window in which I observed, just as much, the reflection of the signs — weak as too outstretched...

And then I don't know why I turn but I did.

It was a presence. A breath on the back of my neck, Aba would have said The tush of my head.

I turned to the boy turning to me he was running, his arms flapping flight shed wildly.

He turned, and the boy met him.

His skin the milk of pigeons, with dark eyes and hair, maybe the earliest dew of a moustache.

Stubbly manna, it tickled, I laugh as much as we kissed or just seemed to.

He hugged me I don't know why I hug him back in return.

Us, we hug tightly. We fall on each other. We feel for one and for others we fall. We feel. And we hug.

Their eyes shut, they squeeze — just like lemons.

And then they explode.

Mind the seeds.

One boy's name was his, the other boy's name was his, too. The same age, then they were ten, near enough. And both are now mine. Equally neither.

But the question's far from where is here, how near from there, without a stir of why.

Answer is, I'm dying.

Pigs, here are only pigs, pigs there, too, they're everywhere. A huge pink hurtling, oink-mad shuttling to Get the treyf out of Jerusalem, Route One's rushed hour to Tel Aviv then the sea to surf on over to Europe. Honk. Rumps backfire. Hynk. Pigs are coming out of the woodwork. Ambulant help. Emergent winged from the grain of void. Honk if you're no longer living. Pigs are flying past me here but it's not just pigs I see before I can't see anymore or won't live: these pigs are pigs with faces, human like the faces that kiss when you've folded your underwear (appropriate drawer) and scream when you haven't and instead you've strewn the little stained white shrouds all over the branching boughs of the widest and only tree in your smallest and only garden: this a man who resembles my teacher Moreh Kulp at the school for the Gifted & Talented also on Tchernichovsky Street (why O why did we have to live right next door?), that a woman who must be or must have been the twin of the one that, a sister of the woman who, the Only a

girl Aba once said was my Aunt was Aunt
ZIforget Zelda until the Queen she came back
north from the Negev and never answered anything about everything that I had wanted and
waited so long to hear until I stopped asking
and thought I knew but didn't these many
many many other — but now the TV's always
off (how even if you'd knot an antenna to the
tailfeathers of a falcon, heaven would get hor-
rendous reception) — pigged people I can't
recognize, don't know and might never, I won't,
but must be nimble enough to hora around as
if my death were my wedding, to jump over just
like that great gymnast Katia Pisetsky tumble-
saulting away from them to avoid being blind-
sided, swiped by them then helplessly
whisked away up into the sky and its vault and
its much vaunted warmth and light that neither
warmed nor did it light, though others say the
very snouts of these pigs flare as if suns themselves in a shine that forces you to feel their
flight and to be burnt by it, remarking upon the
hot puffs to be felt upon the wound of the neck,
pig-exhaust your eyes because my eyes that
have now become sockets can't be opened
again to this gleam this high up and higher, this
glint, this bright coinlike chinging that rings in
my very own ears resounding on my all the
way up this gilded or maybe it's a real solid 24
carat gold ladder I ascend as if I'm walking a

necklace of jingjangling bracelets like those
the Queen always kept clasped around her an-
kles and wrists, this ladder I must, I am ascending now with the whole entire bottom of it,
the foot of it All shod a thousover from whence
I arose becoming dimmed now to the din of
First Responders, archangelic professionals
uniformed all in white, with their protective
masks and their sanitary gloves because to
even see or to touch or to be touched by an entity so holy would mean a life worse than death,
might mean a life lived out on one leg, for one,
without the suck of a lung, for instance or two
or the sponge of a liver, all thanks to the inter-
cession of these Tzadiks Aba always said always with their booties and their beards, their
flightless wings mere flutters of tape that serve
to separate the living from the dead, to protect
the exploded and now ascending from the un-
exploded and unascendant, the seemingly
sudden arrival of onlookers, journalists on-
scene, adulterers and the electrician, all these
dusky sirens that Turn turn turn just like rubies,
those roseate pearls they seem pealing dis-
tantly more and more silent in their twilit set-
tings of silver tarnished so delicately now and
so small that they seem to be cities, Moshav
and Kibbutz and the Multiplex, the Hypermarket with their lots empty for "ample parking"
as seen from this high up and higher heard

until not seen anymore and further deafened forever by the stars that fall and the wails I'm constantly boosting from and climbing, clambering ever fainter from, past the snorting squealing discordant pigs, piglets, sows and tapirs maybe even like from **WITH ATTRAC-TIVE TRICOLOR PLATES**, the illustrations from the KETER encyclopedia set Volumes I through I forget that Aba had given me (ninth birthday) and let me keep in my room up on the seventh highest shelf of the widest and only bookshelf in my bedroom he built the seven shelves with his own two hands like these rungs that I'm reaching at, stretch-straining one to another up on tiptoeing for. Firsthand all the way. To the head.

He's not even sure if it is a true ladder but not thinking this either, because all he knows of it is a single leg, just a single leg is all and with all of its many myriad rungs extending off to one side (east, if), and so far he's unable to discern or even sense a second or any other leg otherwise numbered — but who has the time to count, an end at all to these numinous rungs that for all I know might flow out on forever, growing weaker and weaker, and weaker forever on, less like rungs more like rungs of water, as if streams through utter nothingness to step splash down into and fall through for-

ever, and so I cleave, cling tight to the one and only leg, and climb, just climb the ladder I found climbing abandoned by anyone else inside the emptied footloose shoe store: indeed, this ladder was the grown-up, morphed-around just like on the TV ladder of the small step-stair step-ladder (actually three-step-ladder) the employees of the shoe store used to use to grab up their merchandise, grubbing all of the different sizes and shades from the higher than infinite shelves. Whenever I opened my eyes and found myself alone and what's more possibly, probably, dead I walked into the shoe store — small yet sepulchral bells hung like heads, as if the speaking of tongues had been emptied from the very innards of chimes sounding hallowedly hollow, Titus-like tintinnabulation of timbrel to sentinel my entrance (through the no glass that was left, past strewn dispersion everywhere amid empty shoes, estrays flung far from soulmates and) — walked into the shoe store as if to find there Aba and the Queen but they weren't here and I was because actually nobody was, then finding this ladder grown up right in front of me like the stalk of a skyscraper I don't know why I began to ascend but I did, just like Spideyman I don't know why I ascended but I have and that by the first rung pitched at the height of the roof I scaled how I'll never know why I found the ladder flowing up ever higher, up and up into sky up and then into void void of void. Stratospheric and further beyond into nothingness, and its absence, which is nothing if it's not the very proof of nothingness just through the hole blown into the blown up roof of the shoe store.

Now that he has made his ascent, he is wrong. In the wrong. Being dead, he's correct. But being dead where he is, he's in error. Incorrectly mistaken. Not him but here is what's wrong, all wrong, because everything about this heaven is wrong, and the timing of it, too, for him, for now and for here.

Pigs tried to take me unto their squigglies, their hypnotically spiraling tails and their hairy and rotting though seemingly citric oiled flanks, exposed hunks of bunched phosphorescent bone to hug tight with your thighs tightened against the grease of the wind, oinked me to grab on, snouted me out to hold on and hold tight, offering me to ride them out to wherever their flights might end, terminus, maybe hoping I'd guide them to safer, smoother landings. But I ignored them because of climbing, climbing is enough.

Yes, I'm not as Dummmmmmmmkopf as Aba he once said and then apologized more

for the Queen than to me: I know I am deader
than dead. And that the boy whoever he is,
whoever he was went and exploded me because he was one of them and I one of mine.
And maybe still am or no. My parents are dead,
too. Perhaps. They were also of mine. As the
boy's parents were most definitely one of his,
most probably are. And that they were one of
his made him one of his, still makes and blah
blah. In return. Maybe it's because he hugged
me, and so tightly, that I'm here. He squeezed
me in with him, possible. Like just managed to.
Embrace it. But here, which is in the wrong
heaven. His. Theirs and not mine. A heaven of
others, Not for me.

He expects me to do something I can't.

Though some appeal, most won't.

Politics were always on the radio when I
was alive. Whenever we listened to politics
were on the radio Kol Israel 98.4 on your FM
dial all I ever heard was the sound of goat.
Sound of tragedy the sound of goat. Radio said
Goat and I listened. Bleat bleated to bleat in
bleat at bleat, bleats bleat of bleat and baa
baaa bleating. Hungry goat senseless as goat
as hungry but when I listened it was always
with a full stomach (An empty head). Why I say
politics is that I want to say goat, and why I say

goat is that the radio waves traveled through the air and past me (INFO, from *Informashun*, is the word in American, an acquirement thanks to my dictionary, ALCALAY shelved alongside my encyclopedia set), radio waves announcing the death of a boy named the same as I'd been back then — and the deaths of his parents, too, I think I heard and that of others and their parents and static, István Jontovics, 72, Raya Malesa, 23 — but the radio waves that sounded to me as if the sounding of goats they bounced off the pigs that were flying then bounced, rebounded, redounded, were deflected, repelled, ricocheted, shuttle-shunted, became babbled bebabbled and so all the while ascending the ladder, its rungs, I heard my name, I am sure of it — and many other names, as well, such as those of Nir Pershits, 32, Einat Yavin, "only 18" — but that I heard them all strange, all goatish or goatified and the sounds further said upside down, outside in. But how I knew, how finally *uti possidetis* as Aba used to say — wrongly— in the Latin of our *terra nullius* he said Aelia Capitolina if you know it I knew and know I was and am really truly totally dead Absolutely so is that at the very summit of the ladder (or just on an amazingly huge, filled with heaven rung and me, I'm none the wiser) I found myself once again in Jerusalem, my home in Jerusalem and what's more in

Jerusalem on its Tchernichovsky Street, the
street of my house (our apartment), the street
of my school with the shoe store adjacent (the
toy store was always "just around the corner"),
and what's worse once again in front of the
shoe store itself and In good repair as if the
ladder had ascended up into the air and its
space only to emerge through a merely mun-
dane sewer just now steaming open, the mist
now listing my stagger onto the street I had
only just left in the proverbial down below. It
was strange. And the same. Except that here
the shoes were back in their boxes. The boxes
were back on their shelves. Intact, the window
was, too. Though alone.

I came closer to the window as the window
came closer to me, on the heels of the shoes on
display within the sheen of its glass, my reflection. As I have said, my parents weren't there.
As It has been said, seemingly no one was
though only at first. It was then that I walked up
to my very own me, its reflection dim in the
dark but of form there was more than enough.
To be shocked like the once I stuck my sucked
thumb into the socket at the wall under the
table in the kitchen, stuck my tongue in the
What Happened To Your Pants? which was what
the Queen always asked me who then turned
around to look down at his hands in all privacy.

They were hands even private: one palm up, one palm down, one half always unknowable. Unknown, I touched my nose with a knuckle. It was a nose, the one I got from Aba's mother, my grandAba's Queen and a knuckle. I turned again wildly as if to shatter the window of the shoe store and there it was three times thrice undeniable. The It was my face full open to seep. A squishy squashed olive from the tallest and only tree in our largest and only garden. Out back with the benches and bush. A pond small and dry. To have nails instead of features, dimples their heads, the lineaments of my face each a pure length of rust, nails and their heads bowed reverently as if hammered by hate, lowered out my temples just then shook with a laughter. My tongue burned. I couldn't contain myself. Let it all hang out. Spill it, Yon. It was a hole in my stomach I then bowed forward to — taking three steps back from the reflection to accommodate my goggle — a jaggedly pulsing hole, edged in a heat that was furious, through which my eyeless sockets first beheld the first fully naked naked woman (no, not even the Queen) I had ever remembered.

SHOES

Shoes. Shoes. Shoes. And Shoes to pair good measure. There were always shoes. Never shoe. No one in my house (meaning in our apartment on Tchernichovsky Street, which Aba always called The Road That Should Have Been Named After Bialik) had ever said Shoe. Had never said I can't find a shoe. Had never said I lost my shoe. As in just the word. Like singularly all alone. Or even Where the EXBLEEPLE-TIVE is my shoe? Asked Have you ever seen, smelled or touched its pleather, tasted your own foot in your mouth and its shoe along with it, heard it sneaker from behind an approach? And never when you've decompressed, becalmed yourself enough to ask What have you done with my shoe? Or Where has my shoe walked off to? Ever. Shoes were to be kept together, preferably, to the Queen, to be kept tied together, two shoelaces — or are they four? or one? — left knotted, strangling each other until the morning of our fingers would worry them separate, apart. Loose and achy.

Laces to lie exhausted upon the lemonmopped
linoleum gasping for air. Limp, and then finally
— maybe once a season for me when I was
then living and then growing, maybe only
every five, six or even every ten or so years for
Aba and the Queen — when they died they
would be tied together again, then bagged to
go to the Poor. In bags of plastic brought home
from the Mega Hypermarket built atop the
grave of Pierre Koenig I never knew who he
was until now though I knew Pierre Koenig
Street. A General vs. the Nazis in Africa then
the Poor, wherever they were and whoever, too,
as I never knew the Poor but the Poor knew my
shoes. Made for Kazakh feet. For Ethiopian feet
on a boy probably three years younger than I,
once was. For whom they'd still be small, tight
and pinching. A shoe for their foot, the Poor's:
one huge hungry, shoe-sucking, lace-slurping
monster with an xillion stomp-tromping feet.

My son should study Aba always said My
son should study the podiatry of wandering, All
of the pedestrian interpretations of Exodus and
then laughed until the Queen slapped him on
the scapulate, his back as broad as that of an
ox. But I at not ten nonyears had had the opportunity to study nothing at all until the first
fully naked girl who was also the first totally
nude woman I had ever remembered, beheld

for the first outside the celestial shoe store stared curiously at my shoes, then knelt down and examined them, sniffed at them and even lightly licked with the quick tip of her tongue engreening in the ether. Then What are they? she asked in it seemed a hundred-thousand voices all trying to say as One, Whose force measured me, knocked me over with Why? and so I rose and then said to her what they were They are shoes I said to her that shoes like these are for feet like these are for walking like this and then to Show not just Tell as Moreh Kulp always said I then walked away from her for ten steps and then to her again another six or seven eager step earnest steps as she nodded but obviously could not understand.

Understand that when Aba had to buy new shoes, was In the market for replacement footwear he said that morning, that that was an event of maybe twice a childhood, once in my life. That's why we were at the site of my death, an event, too, once in my life, a tenth birthday as well, not to forget, but before the toy as I've said — or would they, could they have been toys? — it was shoes as has been said, because yesterday's yesterday a nail had come hungry, toothed flesh. Another pair fit for the Poor, which won't fit. A hundred-hundred shoeboxes upended for my grave, a footstone. Pace through the mourning. But my shoes are still alive Aba had said that morning over coffee for him and tea for the Queen he'd said that his shoes were still living. A potentiality for Resurrection at the very least. Not your shoes the Queen "was always right," had to be, said that his shoes were Sick, terminally. Flatlining, from blip blip bleep to one long sheep. Arches fallen in, not sandstone but Aba's. And then the sheep, the lamb, the spotless calf that was me, the healthiest one, and the whitest. A sheep with an Aba for an Aba who wore dead cows on his feet he walked dead always more.

A knotting of thought. That the heaven my grandAba would say me about was not truly believed in. Probably not. That it was possibly null, in the realm of the not yet existent. And another — as if a scatter of shots. That my parents needed another child like they would have wanted me to survive, Desperately and themselves, too. To pair as if flippers or slippers. They would have saved me if they could but they couldn't have even themselves. Merely parents. Marriage then mating. Overprotective isn't how to be God. You have to live I say walk outside your own house (apartment, I say), your own street (Tchernichovsky), your own Jerusalem city and the world Itself on that wide and open and brightly clear afternoon of summermost waste when Aba said Shoes first, toy later. Have to feel free I say but no there's always a ritual to be observed, an indebt to honor. A blessing in the waiting, two-phrased at the crossroads it lies. Again Shoes Aba said we were In the market for shoes. For him, the Queen insisted we had to get shoes for him because Aba Had walked his old shoes out to nail to salted nail because he'd walked his old souls dead and if he wasn't on his toes then his feet along with them. Soon, the son of enough. Sky the toenail under which he walked them to thin at least they'd agree (Aba had to), the sole of the earth — salted so as nothing would ever again grow from its grave. A coffinless coffin's nail was what was hurting him in his walk from his bedroom, which was theirs, too, through the hallway lined with the photographs — first from the bedroom three black & white, then after the bathroom four more in color who remembers of what besides me or who shot them — and inspect each one, individually, for level hang on his run to the bathroom where he'd spend they seemed like hours Resting his eyes on the newspaper the Queen'd slipped under the door a moment after its arrival much much much earlier when the large print was understood by her to be explained away to me later after I woke up from school (to which I walked, terribly, next door and encroaching, only ten

shoelengths down Tchernichovsky Street),
then walked from the bathroom through the
hallway back to his bedroom, which was theirs
to dress leaving the bathroom Under the guard
of his stench, which the Queen always hated, or
else just said she did but which I always found
invitingly pleasant, nose-warming, congenially
flushing of the congenital sinus, then rushed
back from his bedroom to the bathroom for a
less timely sitting in his Reek the Queen always
said after which he'd walk again through the
hallway again and further now down to the
kitchen down where he sat for the breakfast the
Queen always made at which he ate and drank
coffee and café while he read the black of the
paper (the SPORTS the ARTS, the ARTS again)
as the Queen after serving Aba and then me
and only after us then serving herself she read
the front of the paper again, which are the
HEADLINES, which tell the importance of the
day or of yesterday and what will not happen
now or cannot ever hope upon hopes happen
again then to walk through the hallway from the
kitchen to the front door where he walked right
into his shoes waiting there on the mat that said
the word SHALOM we would always wipe our
feet in our shoes on and just step all over,
opened the front door and then a walk Out with
a kiss for each of us but the Queen's on one
cheek of two sumptuously risen Sabbath loaves

despite the day of the week though mine was always on my forehead, on the head even then growing out of my head and right out the front door but out of which what walking now and where I did not know exactly, precisely, not to the step this walking the Queen said All over the whole world Creationdom and Why do you do that to yourself? was what she'd always ask Why don't you take a staff position at the Symphony Philharmonic Orchestra? or at the Opera? Aba would always answer her by saying that he had had enough opera at home Particularly Straussified, Richard and so a Freelancer he was a true Freelancer and to remain a true Freelancer as opposed to a Staff Jobber because he was a tuner, he was a piano tuner Aba always said I don't want to tune the same pianos month after month, moon in and moon out, that I want to tune different pianos, and as many as possible, to redeem, to save as many as possible, pianos, that that's the job of a piano tuner Aba always said meaning he often joked A failed pianist then the Queen would stare him evil then hug him tight (but we didn't have a piano in our apartment on Tchernichovsky Street because Aba wouldn't allow a Big black cancer noise to interfere with his life Aba once said and I just now remember that my Aba he once also told me that When two strings are mathematically perfectly in

tune they actually sound discordant. And that
The job of a piano tuner is to tune a piano, Aba
once said, the strings of a piano, Aba once said,
intentionally discordant, knowledgeably dis-
sonant, slightly Aba once said ever so slightly
and that only then will all the strings sound as
they should — when the hammers come crash-
pedaling down — In perfect, total harmony
Aba once said Which Aba then added is of
course only our perception of —), but after the
Queen hugged him tightly, enabled his en-
abling then let him go, Out, let him loose for a
kiss once again on the other loaved cheek as if
to demonstrate her sympathy with his empathy
and the both of their last, I did not know where
he went (and whether or not the Queen's
cheeks went there with him, as I'd always leave
for school alongside my Aba, who'd leave me
at the school halfway down Tchernichovsky
Street on his way off to wherever It was), rather
I knew that he went to the Symphony Philharmonic Orchestra and to piano showrooms and
music stores throughout Jerusalem and even
greater Tel Aviv and to grandQueens' attics
and basements and cellars and to hospitals
and schools and theaters and fancy Frenchtalian restaurants and also though not as much as
I think he wanted to to the Opera and the Ballet and to the Conservatory or Conservatories,
but I had never been to any of those places, not

to the Philharmonic neither to piano showrooms nor to music stores and all my
grandQueens all my grandQueens were As
dead as music as my Aba used to say and our
apartment on Tchernichovsky Street though it
had a garden and its tree did not have an attic
or a basement or even a cellar and thank God
I've never been in the hospital (though school
is school, and next door at that, five shoelengths away if I didn't do my homework) but
then neither have I ever been to the theater
neither Yiddish nor Shakespearean nor to
fancy Frenchtalian restaurants as starry as the
skies of al-Khwarizmi let's say or the Strauss
Opera or the Stravinsky – Tchaikovsky Ballet,
or the Conservatory of Conservatories there to
clap-clap Concertvatories because Aba he
wanted me to be a lawyer or a professor of History, Semantics or and to speak his parent's
language, which was German at the University
Aba also walked to to tune — walking himself
like a tuned string Aba once said he Walked
around loosening, slackening throughout the
day then tightening up to pure gut again
nearer to home, to his truest pitch at the corner
of Tchernichovsky & — then walked from the
University to the shvitz and then after, walked
to his friend Tannenbaum's house, which was a
real house and not just an apartment three
floors, three bedrooms and two bathrooms with

An open kitchen the Queen would always say
when she was jealous for A moment of peace,
a cup of coffee or maybe a nip of vodka with
slivovitz after which he'd walk all the way back
home to Tchernichovsky Street and our apartment building outside of which I'd wait in the
doorway and always impatiently for him to
pick me up for our every Sunday afternoon
walk into the Old City of Jerusalem, which was
entered always through the Jaffa Gate past
David the King about whom Aba once told me
that in 1889 he said I think it was once in 1898
I think that's when this rampart was demol-
ished, it was destroyed and the moat that used
to poison around it filled up to prepare for the
arrival For the triumphant arrival Aba had said
of Kaiser Wilhelm II as a guest of the Sultan of
Turkey And so that's the huge hole in the wall
Aba once said as we walked into the Old City,
the huge gaping void in the high sun of wall all
about Herod and the three towers of Phasael,
Mariamne and Hippicus Aba said as we
walked in deeper into the Old City and further,
into the spiced hustle, the huddled deal-doing,
zoom in on the see-sighting, but then instead
of further history, which is further explanation
further enlightenment or illumination abruptly
Aba said this once to Ignore all that trash
(though he used a much stronger word), Ignore
all this rubble, these names and their dates that

are only the many other names we use to indi-
viduate indivisible Time, Yoni, save them for
later, which is never, If not now, when, my little
Rav Hillel today (which was the first day before
the shoe store, and so the last day before the
last Monday of life for me, for him and for his
shoes as the nail was even now gnawing up) I
want you Aba said wincing To observe all these
tourists and only the tourists as we walked as
Aba then talked Observe all these tourists but
don't sit in judgment of them just you remove
yourself, he said Stand still at a distance that
comes from being native to a world this FOUL
LANGUAGE wonderful, Yon, and take all of it in:
the French and the German, Yon, always the
youngest Germans Germany can afford to ex-
port, two rows of ten each with matching yel-
low-trimmed tote bags, the umbrella-wielding
Italianevs with their compact designer umbrellas for their umbrellas and then you have
the Polishers, just look at that group of tiny Polisher nuns being shepherded past, this herd of
miniature nun-donkeys, Parvenu parvum don't
you think, Yo? all these donkeys being ridden
by all those midgetized, glandular-problem
nuns as if in A defensive maneuver against this
oncoming phalanx of teenage Greekskis, Mind
your step, each face of theirs as if the floor of
an obsolete oil press being rolled Their eyes
the stomping of grapes, Yon, and don't forget

to bow to the Britishate with their cement teeth
and their concrete molars being guided past
us by an American as we walked Aba and I
holding hands with the Australians and the
Japanese, the Koreans (God, what ideas do they
have? Aba asked) and the Americans, yes,
God, look at the Americans as we walked Aba
and I with my face nuzzled deep in his under-
arm-pit, soaking up all the Tannenbaum's
vodka with a W on its label Aba was sweating
the smell of rotting prehistoric Aba said Pleis-
tocene fish the street always paved our
tongues with to then lick at our lips, yes, the
American, Yoni, Observe the Americans was
what Aba then said: for example, their fat, it
simply obliterates any waist, it quite simply ab-
solves the figure of the human of form And then
their intentions, for instance, which are as immaculate as their collective and yet anony-
mous conscience, which is unconscionable,
Aba said, Like just see how many T-shirts they
buy, Yoni! Enumerate them! T-shirt after T-shirt,
after shirt after cruciform tee all in the shape
of the Jew we once crucified up on that hill at
which Aba then pointed a finger of his as if ac-
cusing the very set of the sun All for them and
for all their relations all their unshapely fat actually unshaped at all Aba said Flabelliform
bodies, the Father, the Son and the Globoid
God! how many bodies do Americans have?

how many bodies does it take to make one
American? Aba asked, while the one body
here is out touring Jerusalem, the Cardo, the
Armenian Quarter, the Holy Sepulcher and its
Church, another body's left back home building missiles and some other body's lined up at
the local kindergarten to vote and yet another
body's stuck in neutral in the drive-in-and-see-
thru, or out basking on the southernmost
beach in central Florida or else pressed up
against Minnie Mouse's plasticine nippless-
ness Aba said That must be why they need so
many T-shirts, this must be what they need
them for all of these bodies, for all of their bodies All of them going every which way all at
once, That's why they hoard them then compliment each other on them the shirts in an America in which it's not polite to compliment a
fellow American on his or especially her body
or bodies on threat of let's say prosecution in-
carceration Corporal slash Capital Punishment
Aba said Mister Jonathan Pollard but in which
it's more than permissible to compliment them
on their T-shirt or shirts Aba said And just hear
them, Yon, will you? just listen to them and you
Yon can save yourself all the money in the universe on all of those Hollywood movies, you
can pick up on All that dialogue the ropes knotted off to the tropes just by listening in and
then smell them, Yon: smellessness, deodor-

ized, they have no whiff whatsoever, they're
without any scent at all as if they're not merely
animals just like everyone else, like me Aba
said or like you Or else as if the season — second — of spring If you can imagine it Aba
asked lasting a whole year and around again
into yet another spring Aba said They smell
like a thousand months of a million moons of
the month of Adar two months ago and its
Purim until the world just pops fat out of its box
on the calendar on the wall in the kitchen Aba
said to me As if all the days of Nisan and their
Aba said Pesadich nights had been sent spin-
ning down into his mouth for him to laugh them
down into himself Aba laughed his laugh again
and again until we had reached the Kotel at
which my Aba's laugh became a light hack
(despite the walk, he always smoked, NO-
BLESSE AMERICAN BLUES and the occasional
occasionally stinky cheroot when not in the
presence of the Queen) then became his deep
wheeze I thought it was until I realized his
laugh had turned in his gut to spring up
through his throat into a seriousness I'd never
previously known Aba then hazarded with the
heaviest of lips, until his Laugh Laugh & Laugh
had turned and almost imperceptibly into the
word *MA-A-RAV* was what Aba said in the language we used to speak together whenever we
spoke Aba said *MA-A-RAV* ever so faintly again

and again he said *MA-A-RAV*, which means in every language *WEST* Aba said *WEST WEST WEST WEST WEST.*

NAKEDNESS

akedness is the formlessness of the void. In the Genesis of the Torah, in the first chapter of the first book of the first and only Torah (if only in the second "sentence," perhaps), existence is described as being without form and void. And yet as beingness, still. This means that existence before Creation was naked. And that Creation was a covering of this nakedness. Modesty, only. I say this because here where I find myself is naked. Here there is totally nude. Though I would like to think I share not much with those I encounter here I must admit we are all formless voids, too. O naked us! Pity the nude, though I'm shod and self-pitied. Why we are all formless voids is because we have all long since surrendered — whether willingly or not — any pretense toward individuality. Freeing our souls has meant losing them. Forever, I mean.

I find here I am assigned eighteen mothers. As round and as pure as ostrich eggs, they are as round and as pure as the eggs of os-

triches are my eighteen mothers and more,
maybe more (I only say eighteen because only
that means them all). Ostrich eggs burst fat
filled with fat white grapes filled fat with enormous opalescent pearls or are they ostrich
eggs I don't know, I'm not sure. Eighteen eyes
white around but black in the middle, Cancer
Aba would have said if he wasn't dead, living in
another heaven, I hope. It is convenient that in
this Heaven we all speak or rather we all understand the same language or at least I understand what they let said to me, what It does
and it all sounds — almost — like the tongue of
America. Anyway, all here are merely *spoken
through* (and Queen Houri supports this, no,
she embodies), and so our mouths open only
to allow a saying that has nothing to do with the
apparently individual or previously individu-
ated entity doing the saying, mouthing and
blah blah who says. Not the man named Mohammed, who is shut up now in perpetuity, and
for It (that is, the man named Mohammed is
shut up, not his mouth). Rather the One always
saying the saying through them, through the
man named Mohammed then through them, by
which I mean through us and through me (and
does Mohammed picky & choosey through like
the Queen with me and the front of the newspaper?), that first sayer of sayings is said to be
an entity that has been named by Who or an

entity that has named Itself Allah. It is not to Allah however that we, meaning I should address my appeal. I find myself saying this: it is not befitting Allah that Its words should be flung back at It. In your face. As if beets I'll never eat. I remember. Like shoes to the Poor.

As these mothers, my mothers, have no individual names or ever had, or at least refused them and still do, they asked me all as One — and so as nothing and so as no one— and without saying anything at all to say to them Houri. A name. We are a virgin is what they said without saying and I suppose they knew that I was one, too. We would be your lover and remain virgin forever they said but soon knew — through Allah? through the man named Mohammed? — that I needed a Queen more, a Queen and more: a Queen who is also her own attendants, her court and her courtiers, her subjects and guard.

My Queen is so naked. Here this nakedness seems to be the height of modesty. But, to demur: It's that I feel I must say this is possibly not what their heaven, their Pardes or Paradise, is like (the sand above the sand, the sand below the sand, the sand in the dunes), saying this possibly only because I say I do not belong here and so this is how I perceive it.

Listen. When I ask them are you my mother? or will you be my mother? one says Yes, another says Do you want me to be, a third says Only if you want to be my son, and yet another Only if you will be my son, and a fifth If that is who I am, and a sixth If that is who you want me to be, and a seventh If that is how I can best serve you, and an eighth If that is how I can best be served, and another If that is who I was, and another If that is who I am not, was not and another If your father is God, and another (Only) if your father is not God and blah blah, and that all of these promises, these blessings and curses course out, all at once and all saying the same if in words that appear to oppose — as if their very answers were only random words of a sustained prophecy fled into sound, propheticules just flowing out of them and through them like the fulminant foamings of watery wine: out from between their wide parted rubies that mouth these long reaches of let's say tentacle, of binding fringe, of curly lock these endless shafts of air that serve to vibrate a pitch in the air sympathetically all these pitches all wavering as if the rib of a leaf in a storm or the quivering cord by which sustenance would come up from the womb, though I still hear them now in my memory and will forever more as strings not of puppets or of universes but of an enormous piano emanating

from the very massing of their mouths — the
huge grands Aba used to work on when he
wasn't called over to fix and tune a
grandQueen's fungiform upright — a huge
sky-wide, sky-long piano is what I heard and
still hear that was strung with strings that were
invisible, are like hot air gone gusted not only
from their very mouths but also as if from their
always moist, tuned, tightening and loosening
vaginas, from their also always moist, tuned
and tuning, tightening and loosening anuses
and nostrils and even from the very mutilated
womb of their navels, an A 440 Hz streaming
out from their stomachs at the deforming scar
of their umbilici, this A down lower an octave
below the middle of All and of everything, A
the highest string of the *Cello entry from behind pain:* which was Aba's favorite poem the
Queen once played fluming *von hinter dem
Schmerz:* out from between the cleaved halves
of their ebony rubies, studded with beryl and
carbuncle and all at once coursing out in an
enormous candling then wicked apart into
plaits then strands of their hair to braid with the
braids then braiding and then those braids all
wrapping into a bow of one enormously strong
length of flame sounding deep and too low
maybe even for any perception except that of
rabid dogs on fire, a ray of molten brass it then
seemed to part the iron clouds that would rain

down nails to sound dumb pluck strung out to my own imperfection, out to the exploded hole in me in a too deep thrumming low rumble that seemed to harden into the pipe of an organ, into a diapason of thread knotted to a needle of only an eye, the vibration of the jagged wound in my stomach sounding a hollow note pitched so terribly beyond the All as to blow the world entire back all the way to void again, the universe crumbling, walls tumbling around the city limits of Jericho where I've never been before but an Uncle of mine Alex and the glass he brought back, the Bohemian crystal from the vacation years he took to Prague, the MOSER in our glassed pantries back home (back apartment) on Tchernichovsky Street, Jerusalem, all spidering into a web that was also, it seemed, the constrictive coil of an enormous serpent and its even more enormous hiss giving way only to silence, totally pure silence and still, the truest void though still unnamed and formless. Naked, too. And nude.

This was how their saying was said to me, or at least how I then heard it.

I say this is maybe only how I perceive it was heard, then heard it myself, because it seems I am wrong even here, mistaken even in the wrong heaven: it seems that the Queen is actually clothed, or more accurately that all of her clothing, from the veils that admitted only her eyes down to the sandy hems of her garments, actually comprised her naked and nakedness, and further that her nude was only the accumulation, was merely the layering of these garments that are more like winds composed only of let's say silky leaf that blow cool the heads hanging heavy from the boughs and their branches of the Tree under which they all sit. Under the Tree that actually grew them, a Tree that fruits virgins: first secreting their heads, then their fruited fluted columnarly delicate necks, the breasts blossom, the stomach rounds and its navel stems, the vagina expectedly blooms until, so heavy, they fall float to the ground to sit around the Tree with their sisters.

This Queen, this total massing of women, though they are virgins, is no substitute for the Queen who is immensely beautiful and was. Because there is one flaw here that cannot escape — because it cannot bear — notice even in heaven, even in a heaven that is wrong, indeed a flaw that might be "the very thing" that makes them sisters, their relative scar: because when a virgin falls from the tree, having hung upside down for a longer time than any alive could ever hope to measure, with her own, to span, with her own, the virgin falls suddenly, al-

most unaware, or as if consciousness — hers —
didn't exist until this fall to the ground, which
is sand. And they hit. And so unknowing, unaware, the virgin falls with no ability or else, if
you prefer, acknowledged forewarning to protect herself, and so with no help, inexplicably
or not, from her sisters, invariably falls hard, a
fruit bruised, even smashes herself, on the fa-
natically protruding root structure of the tree,
on the razor-edged, manicured nails of her sisters, upon the rocks that star the tree's trunk,
and so each virgin, each of these sisters that
are all of them a mother, just as much, has a
flaw and will always: a dune on her nose, a gash
royally smashed upon her forehead, a scar
piercing the ear to the lip (it's a long fall, taller
than ten times to what I would've grown), a
poked in eye or inverted nipple, a caesari-
antype incision inflicted by a single, wind-
sharpened blade of grass and blah blah, all
imperfections, blemishes on these most un-
cowlike of creatures (women in shape, not in
manners), which the Queen, my true Queen
dead and in the heaven of her own belief,
would have frowned a dark rainbow upon, be-
tokening a covenant of disapproval and
whether rightly or wrongly thought these phys-
ical imperfections a sign, a manifestation of an
immemorial inner problem, the gradual ema-
nation of a spiritual decay, a disease that would

eat the woman alive, the women, eventually, and then any man she or they might ever have touched.

I am in the wrong heaven I said to Queen Houri.

As I walked in strange to them shoes around and around the trunk of the Tree around and around their seemingly infinite ring (or at least never remembering one of them the women twice in thrice and more around) and around the trunk of the tree and said to them I was embraced then exploded into this paradise that is yours and not mine, that I do not belong here because you say I don't belong here (I listened) blah blah, and that I am only I because you are you.

Why? Queen Houri asked as one.

Why not become one of us?

And as the sound of the question stretched across their seemingly infinite mouths, the softly grown heads of the tree shook the question to the ground as if No.

Yes — asked the virgins, their sisters grown from the Tree, why disappointed?

Just as death is a renunciation of life, they said without saying to me I have only now to renounce that that's survived it. Me. But you can't.

Why bitch? Aba would ask.

He meant the Queen would say Why complain?

But Queen Houri, the full grown virgins to ripeness, picked up the rocks penning in their ring (which turned to stone in their hands), and with them pelted the heads and the partiformed faces of their becoming sisters because these still growing, nascent virgins are not only not permitted to say anything but, further, are prohibited from even eavesdropping upon any of the saying of their fully formed, all-realized sisters below much as Aba he once said That other people believe if you eavesdrop on (which?) heaven God throws down flaming stars aimed at your head, which in his case would be mine now exploded. But these rocks and stones and even fluorescent pebbles and gravel like from the fishbowl where I kept Dag and the other Dag after the first Dag died and we flushed him away, down deep into Aba's oozy smell, into the woozy wake of his turds these hot, hard and dirty implements are aimed not only at the soft of their heads, the ears of those who could and so would listen in

— as if they could help it, this happy patron-
ization of their newfound protrusions — but are
aimed also at their bodies, at their own lesser
wet voids, everywhere and so maybe it is from
this very hurling and lobbing that their flaws
exist but perhaps are only evident, meaning to
us, when these virgins hit ground. And as hard
as virgins. And are thusly explained, said so
away.

None of this was explained neither was
said to me as one woman, a part of Queen
Houri — a toe of the Queen, I like to think, a
majestic thumb, also I might remember the one
who arose from the midst of her sisters to Meet
& Greet me upon my arrival at the laddertop
shoe store — arose to escort me now right out
of the Jerusalem Above and its valleys, the sand
beyond the sands beyond the city limits, and
all the way to a Fountain because my questions
then seemed to her, as it must have, too, to
them, quite physically thirst and the water to
be obtained there and there only — have I
mentioned that most of this heaven is quite obviously a desert? — would answer all for me,
questioned. Please I said as the Queen would
have had me say Thanks. Would quench or so
it's said, and it was. But as this full woman
thumb toe escorted me up and down dunes,
around and around dunes and then in and out

of the valleys sanding between them, as she
with we walked further and further away from
the remainder of the Queen that is Houri — she
unshod, me in my shoes so as not to lay skin
upon foreign sand — she grew more and more
naked, more and more whisperweight, trans-
parent and, after a time I could not ever hope to
translate to you even if I had half of Time in
which to do it, I turned around at the very top of
a dune and saw the previous dune through her,
then saw her no more.

With her disappearance I could not hope
to find the Fountain but shade.

Up ahead, after walking longingly, was
shade but a curious shade of it: a shade with
nothing in evidence to produce the shade, with
no shading presence, no entity of shade dis-
cernible between the shade, which was the de-
lineated darkness upon the sand all of one
infinite grain, and the immaculate golden plate
above that served up nothing at all. Save light
and warmth unfulfilling. I stood in this shade
shaded by nothing and then I lay and then I
slept, I must have slept and when I awoke there
was no shade but I was under the wide, long-
ribbed leaves of another tree. However its
leaves, which were generous fronds of palm,
provided none of the shade I had so enjoyed

previously: the setting of the golden plate pro-
ceeded on its natural strength unabated, and it
was as if the shards of the plate now smashed
on the knife of the horizon had stuck through
the palms, had pierced them through and so
pierced me, too, stigmatic under this element
of shade that provided none, having no purpose for any incarnation but its own. An unim-
peding impediment. A stumble without snare.
And that after the golden plate smashed then
ashed away to the white darkness of smoke I
slept again and did not dream of the Queen,
neither of Houri, but instead of an unmanned
caravan of approximately let n equal x thousand nursing camels or pregnant that were approaching me from afar (the direction from
which they were arriving I'd titled Fast, the
other I would name Fleet), their humps as
dunes dispossessing themselves of their earth
and moving on, always, a sandscape perpetu-
ally in motion so as to seem only the same
again and again — repetition as ritual, wandering the only, which is favored, method of
stasis, the Latinate *nunc* as Aba always said
Whether permanens or stans — what it was
was just camel after camel after camel after all
of them, all just bobbing like buoys up and
down as if lifejackets made exclusively for the
salvation of hunchbacked Ukrainian cleaning-
women down and up on the driest, most arid,

landed sea imaginable — such was this dreaming of the camels approaching and always approaching as if when they'd ultimately
approach, finally arrive, then and only then
would I finally awake, knowing this to be the
Truth of the True as it's said and that they
seemed as if they'd never, will never approach,
until they actually had approached, finally, arrived and laid down in the darkness in no
shade just in front of me, in a circle around the
tree providing nothing for no one, folded into a
squat atop their legs of all spindles and there
nosing at one another (much nuzzling of parchment flanks, is what), and so I struggled, fought
against this dream, into waking at the image —
not the mirage — at this the image to be found
reflected down deep in the deepest well of the
mind the recognizance of which should have
signified the end of my dreaming, must have
and must still, but my struggling, all my fight,
was in vain, is: because I would never wake up,
because I wasn't dreaming at all, it wasn't a
dream, it was never a dream and still isn't.

The camel caravan had arrived and I was
awake all the while for all.

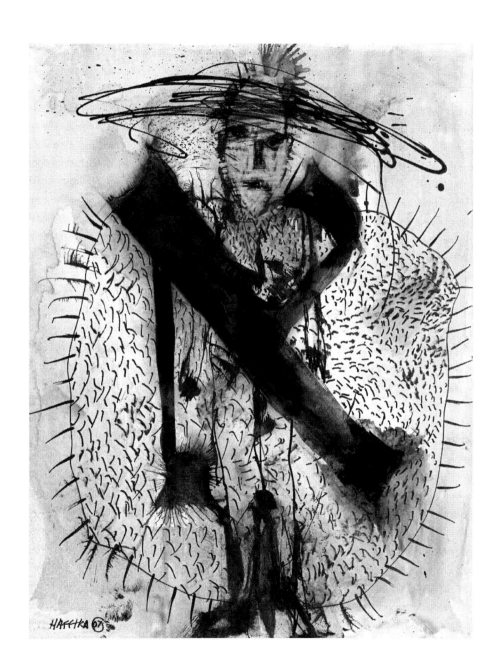

ALEF

I am the ass
they whoever they ever are
would pack with explosives
would burden with
        explosionary material
fertilizer bombs, nail-
packed explosives until
the guards
the security
the patrolling police & the
ordinary everyday citizen
they began beginning and so
they whoever they ever are
instead of packing the explosives atop
me or at my sides in beastlike
breastlike bags
they whoever they ever are
began instead
stuffing
the explosives up inside of me
into my ass and so
stuffing
me full
there is no why
I am relating this
I just am

A PILGRIMAGE

It would seem simple, it would. You go toward the Two Mountains and the Two Mountains come toward you. As they come, you become. You come toward the man and the Man goes toward you. As He comes, He becomes he. Ingathering, he'd honk at the doorway. Aba would make the sound of the horn with his tongue dumbly thrust out of its mouth like a camel's or bird. Shoes, I'd say, I can't find my shoes. I can't find, then I'd find them. He's coming was what Aba would say to the Queen who'd Heard it all before. Me, too. I'm going. I was always late for school, I was always the first one home. Then dinner. You eat your beets and the Queen lets you watch cartoons is how it went. Or the Queen lets you watch cartoons and you've eaten your beets is how it should go. Should have gone, bath, lastly bed. But I never kept that half of the haggle.

Are you coming? one virgin said to another Or is he going with us? all said to each other even as I left them and so all of Queen

Houri said to me and even I said it, too, which is to submit as I set out to seek with the help of their thumb.

Walking, I left.

And submissively long.

The way they said it, it seemed so simple, it would. Any direction to one destination. Every cardinality to a capstone. Shoot an arrow then follow it long. Walk on your hands clad in the gloves of assassins. Go down and submit. But exodus is never that simple.

They were the camels. They had ridden me out to the Fountain at which I drank without quench. They had ridden me out to another fountain, then a third. And still no. Water gushed out my jagged hole, a sprung with no spring. Again and again I explained to them and so to myself what I called just like the Queen called any thousand of hers My predicament What's His Problem What Happened To My Pants, then one camel drew with its foot in the sand a map quickly effaced by the wind. Cloven-over. And so it drew it again, or attempted to, and then again, each time the map only one-ninth, or merely one-seventh, finished, then the erasure from wind. Complete. I'm talking utter. Then two camels

worked on the map, each at an opposite end, and the map was then one-third-finished, or two two-sixths-whole, then again the wind and then nothing. And so three camels and then four, each from its own gusting quarter until the wind again and so finally it took seven of the camels all hoofing it simultaneously to all together complete the map I had by then memorized in whole as I had had it in part. As for why the camels couldn't ride me out there themselves, it wasn't ever proposed. Into never, I left.

Having been directed to the Valley between the Two Mountains, I followed. I was to seek the man named Mohammed. And that there he would help me, It was said He would have to. Transfer me to the afterlife most appropriate to my previous Yes. No questions asked. Having answered none I went. Having substantiated nothing I submitted. This man named Mohammed would rectify this mistake — mine, His, or that of no one, none other. This mistake as unmistaken as all divine, but a rectification had been made necessary still. Not an apology. A mere reparation. Miser it a healing. A whole. Not on faith, to go on desperation.

How does he know a voice said.

It was a gust.

And know this, too. He was scrutinized by the sun. Light and warmth despite day or night was denied me, then granted in showers, in snows the color of ash burnt in ovens. As it is said. And that the sand preserved his tracks as it preserved the trail of none other.

To be here as him is to be hated by even the wind. It is said. Listen to it. Hear it listening. It has been said that in this strangest land he is as much a stranger as It tells him he is.

Still, as the Queen always said It helps to prepare. Never hurts. And so if ever he would find this man named Mohammed he was to say Salaam. And then he was to say his name. Not that the man named Mohammed didn't know his name or His Own but that this ritual was to serve as both a Sign & a Wonder, respectfully speaking, a submission implying in no way the ultimate submission, which is forbidden him though only by himself and by others and, further, that only after this Salaam, My Name Is the man named Mohammed would be obliged to rectify any unmistaken mistake all in a matter of immediacy and without further questions neither answers whether they be Of the Above or terrene (such as reincarnation, resurrection and terrestrially yadda) — how he rehearsed the voice saying through him Salaam, my name

is Jonathan son of Saul A. Schwarzstein he said
into pools reflecting his mouth (thinking thank
God how good it is that in heaven you don't
have to scrub teeth), the words rippling out,
bulls'eyes circling the swell of his Salaam he
said my name is Jonathan son of Saul A. is for
Aba Schwarzstein, Yoni to my Aba he said
who's As dead as the rocks that shine his mouth
with macle as if the stone itself were the very
perspirant tears of the rock hard within, the
swirling water the very sweat of the words
Salaam, my name is Jonathan son of Saul Aba
Schwarzstein and I live at 37 Tchernichovsky
Street, apartment number (#) 3, Jerusalem was
how the Queen had taught him how to get his
way home when he didn't know how he was
getting there or from where and my Aba's telephone number, it's #717736 7-1-seventyseven-
3-6 was how he dressrehearsed the nakedness
of the audience like he did with his role as Pan
Janusz Korczak the lead in last spring's school
play to the terraced tiers of shrubless crags
and the stadiumed shrubs of the crannies that
horizoned the All: the wrinkly knotted faces of
the putrescent trees and the murderous cliffs
with their sharply cleaved crevices that echoed
in return if not his voice then the voice of another he followed as if such horrible pain was
his own — a man with a face hanged spread-

eagled, nailed and thrice, hard, to a severe
flank of mountain not his.

Who are you? I asked the man and the
man said Salaam.

And so I said to the man Alaikum to you
and then the man asked me Who are you?

Jonathan son of Saul Schwarzstein and I
live at 37 Tchernichovsky Street but you can
call me Yoni I said to the man to whom I also
asked among many other things such as Do
you know where the Two Mountains are?
Where are the Two Mountains? Do you know
the man named Mohammed? Where would I
find the man named Mohammed? I asked him
as I told the man my story as an answer and the
millennia behind it.

And so you understand I am a stranger
here in your heaven I said to the man. And so
you understand a mistake has been made I
said to the man. And so you understand I am
walking to the Valley between the Two Mountains to make an appeal. That I am seeking rectification is what. Restitution to the Eden of my
however inherited however believed belief.
Why not. But mostly I just want my parents I
said to the man whom I almost do not now remember as anyone other than me.

It is good I am still able to see you said the man.

And it is good you are able still to be seen.

I asked the man what he meant by that and the man said he had been hanging there thrice nailed to the flank forever and so I asked the man Why? and the man said as if an answer that one serving of the golden plate a raven he liked to think was Noah's — though he said he knew no other — had descended from the knife's edge of the horizon, had plucked out his right eyeball and then flew away. Beaked it up and out with it, so I asked the man Why? and the man said You have a pleasant face, then I asked the man what had he done to incur such a punishment (Alive, I had tried to gaze into the future, he said), this Ravenous wrath and the man then said Now I am waiting for the distant relative of the raven by whom I mean to accuse the dove to fly down and pluck out my other ball for an eye on the day on which I will see no longer. And then the man said to me nothing, merely opened toothlessness, revealed to me the moons of his tonsils as I left him in the direction of the golden plate, which was yet again serving up nothing at all.

In heaven, even — dusk, the arrival of night.

And so I walked long. Thanking all the while I had thought to take a pair of new shoes with me upon my ascent, and thinking that if I had ascended up here wearing my old shoes — which, after all, weren't really that old — I would have been walking around unshod now or at least in destroyed shoes forever and longer (have I neglected to mention I "redeemed" a new pair and just my size just prior to my ascent, my meeting and greeting of Houri? and if so, I repent — if it makes any difference, I tried to grab the least expensive, grub those that would be the least missed). Not that I needed shoes for this earth or rather it's that the earth of this heaven is incredibly soft, tender, in feeling much like laying your hands upon the stomach of a living human as enormously fat as is Uncle Alex in respiration and perhaps lightly perspiring after a full dinner of the Queen's because the Queen always said he was Too fat to have a Queen of his own. Which was mean. She was his sister.

However my new shoes did prove useful — and, at the same time, met their end — as I approached what appeared to be a stream of last light. A dying ray, I walked longer and to it, as there did not seem any way or route around it or over. Indeed, it was a stream, and a stream that had to be crossed, waded through. Dip-

ping my hands in to drink I understood it was honey, which was refreshing both to hunger and thirst, but which was extremely difficult to pass over or through. And so I stepped in because there was no other way. No bridge whether of wood, iron or human laid out across the flow foot to head. And so I stepped down because there was no other way to step but down and my stepping foot, my left in its new left shoe, became stuck in the honey. I was unable to lift my foot and so there was nothing I could do but to step my other right foot new down into the honey as well. Which I did and now both feet in their shoes were stuck fast. Me, too. Mire and I. And the honey wasn't flowing it was hardening. Amberizing. And quickly. I almost lost myself and fell but as I spread out my hands wide as if the wings of a bird protesting its innocence just then two eagles descended and each took a forefinger of mine into its beak and pulled me out, all of me except my new shoes, which I left behind to be stuck in the honey. A sacrifice but in the air the eagles began to dogfight with each other or maybe not fight, but I would say Will: rather one wanted to fly me one way and the other wanted to fly with me another and that they made this quite evident to me as if asking me to decide for them and so for me but if I did or would then how would I be able to communicate my decision to them and for, by their pulling me apart in two different directions that were always the opposite (I son of Saul, no son of Solomon) — one away to one edge of the golden plate and the other away to the other edge of the golden plate that is edgeless, but not wanting in the least to displease, to disappoint either and so to get myself ripped then into two living halves who would probably, that far apart, never meet again and join together in famished Farmisht fraternity for the meal once known as Time For Dinner I kept myself as still as inhumanly possible and so allowed them to pull me and tug me zigzaggingly Zephyrusly though never quite gently east to westward if all over the sky and its vault until I had had enough of what I say was indescribable pain and so wrenched them hard both down to the ground, pointing my forefingers as if the accusations of the two witnesses that are required by the Talmud Aba always invoked to two far and high dunes and there willing my strength to my arms to hurl them both down even unto the two dunes, one eagle to each with me nested in the valley between where I landed unharmed though they were killed by the impact.

Brushing sand from himself he gathered the killed eagles and walked longer on a wick

of smoke and also to its source, which he sensed originating "within walking distance." It was a fire in a pit bound by tires and at it there was a boy of his own same age but sitting or lying relaxed. He offered the boy his eagles to eat as a meal and so the boy wrapped the eagles in his headdress that would not burn and buried them under the sand under the fire that apparently required no logs or sticks or twigs nor the tinder of HEADLINES.

Our meal will be ready soon the boy said.

I asked the boy Who are you?

I'm hungry.

Me, too.

And then the boy said he was a boy who had died.

I asked the boy how he had died and the boy asked me the same Who are you?

And so I said to the boy I am apparently a stranger here, a stranger to you in a heaven not mine and the boy asked me then How did you come to be here? and so I said to the boy I had been exploded and the boy asked me then Who exploded you and why? and so I said to the boy that a boy exploded me, a boy about my same age it seemed and yours, too, who had hugged me then exploded me outside of a shoe store located on Tchernichovsky Street in Jerusalem the Third City of at least one Empire as the boy said to me he had once — embraced and — exploded someone or other himself, indeed that that's how he had merited here, by martyring himself he'd earned for his death this life after life and a death that was glorious and so I asked the boy Who? and the boy said to me I don't know and so I asked him again Who was it? and the boy said all he knew was that it was a boy about his own age and mine, too, outside of a shoe store on a street named for a Russian of sorts, he remembered, maybe a Finn the boy said in Jerusalem I'm not sure, though he called it Al Quds (Abul Ala al-Maari Way, he said, maybe it was, a writer, I'm feeling a poet), which is home to Quabbat As-Sakhrah and Al Aqsa meaning the Furthest have I ever been there That far, I asked the boy why as in Why did you do it? and the boy said to me He was not you, do not worry — And he was not you either was what I then said to the boy who said to me then that our meal was now finally ready and that We should wash before we would eat but there was no water to be found, only smoke and a tire.

They ate (in heaven, no food is forbidden), though neither would fill.

As he turned to take leave of the boy the boy said to me Wait a sec.

I asked the boy Why? and the boy said to me You must wait here until I'll return momentarily and so again I asked the boy Why?

And the boy said to me You have provided the meal of the two quailing eagles and so I must provide in return. Understand. Please & thank you. That you have given me a gift and so in return a gift from me is required. You get it. My man. Understand was what the boy said to me and so I said to the boy it's not necessary, none of It is and what's more it is not even wanted I said please don't get angry with me because a wait and a return and its gift however required or merited will only delay me and I must not delay instead I must seek the Two Mountains and I must find the Two Mountains and the Valley between in which I must seek the man named Mohammed and in which I must find the man named Mohammed so as to set everything but everything right, please understand and yes thank you no you. Slap me one. All I have. But by the time I had finished saying my meaning to him the boy had left and was gone. But by the time the boy was beyond

me like the smoke from our fire I found I could
not leave the fire he'd made or had found there
as many multitudinously beastly creatures,
jackals, had by now surrounded the fire and
there prevented my leaving — *they were jackals*, but were odd, emaciated, crescent-shaped
and up on the hindmost legs of their twelve:
they opened their great alabaster jaws to slash
me there to my stand, circling they were closing in on me constantly nearer and tighter, furl-
ing in always as if a scroll of living, sinewy
parchment on which was written I would say in-
scrutable Mishegas (an alphabet of rips, slash-
marks,   self-inflicted   bites,   cuts   and
ingrammatical tears), coming closer ever
closer just to smother me into sustenance,
theirs, until I could stand just in the fire itself
and atop its very flame, which I did knowing I
could survive the fire longer if not by that much
than I could survive, have survived the fifty it
seemed jackals they seemed that were constantly circling me and closing in on me and so
I stood here in the fire that instead of burning
me or further charring the exploded and so already burnt, died underneath me to a pillar
then a wisp of air and all was again dark, ash-
pitch and only the sound the smacking screech
of the jackals, which were manifestations of
their hunger as insatiable as Time, said to me

the jackals still were, where they were still and that I was not theirs, I mean yet.

I stood in the pit ringed with a tire and there awaited the return of the boy.

But just as boys lack so does heaven.

Heaven has no continuity. After before. Heaven has no consequence. No cause of causality. Without let's say Æffect. A covenant broken. An upheaval, overturned twice. For one: After living a life of morality an eternity is necessary in which to become accustomed to amorality. This is why many of the righteous become many of the wicked in heaven, and why they are punished there. Here is why hell, which is as amoral as heaven, hosts more of the righteous than he will encounter anywhere ever.

Morning if you will, the golden plate returned but empty as always.

He walked long and unshod to the Two Mountains to their Valley and so to the man named Mohammed. As he had exhausted the supplies scavenged then packed for him by Queen Houri (willow-pills, gnawable hides, scraps of bark, dried beetles and a small sackling of dust), he was again hungry, thirsty and exhausted now, too, despite passing wonder-

ments now on his way that he had never once
before wondered, and that (and the hunger
and the thirst) (and exhaustion, as well) might
have been why they did him nothing at all: For
one, the calves that dwelt in the abandoned,
enormously abaloneous shells of extinct snails
enriched him to nihil. For another, neither the
rams trump-trumpeting his arrival (rams that
to communicate blow and intake through their
own horns as their sole means of respiration,
horns that in this heaven are attached to these
rams, which are so breathing and so communi-
cating understandably endangered, in the re-
verse of their terrestrial disposition). Nor the
fallen brigade of seemingly just pubescent
boys with wicks set into their nipples, waxen
wicks dribbling a sexual sebum from the dead
middles of their distended areolæ, the wicks
fuselike, seemingly first pubes first braided
then lit — or else, the ancient people desic-
cated to the ostensibly leprous, stuffed with
earth (heaven's provision being the opposite
of terra's: instead of burying a person in the
ground heaven might bury the ground inside
of a person), their arms out legs spread, leak-
ing earth and spitting worms through green
mucous purpling membranes all of them
shouting to him and screaming all at once at
him in a vomitus of pebbles, gravel and dirt
Salaam Salaaam Salaaaam — all this rendering

him no whys, maybe also because his eyes were fixed as ahead as ahead can ever hope to become fixed in a desert: he had sought and he had found the Valley of Nails.

This was the Valley between the Two Mountains that had been going to him as he had been coming to them. In this Valley of Nails the man named Mohammed dwelt, there it was said he was shut up in perpetuity and here forced to the mere saying of sayings as it was said, further that the man named Mohammed would do for him whatever he asked must be done (meaning He would do for him whatever was asked through him as His). Who would right wrong. Who would left right. Who would map the nonexistent. The inextant Who would teach the dead. But was heaven worth, was the true heaven if it ever existed, if It even exists, His heaven I mean worth this descent, such a fall through the Valley of Nails, of rusty, bent battered nails, of all these old oxidized, dead senseless, head-hammered to wilting nails all blood-caked, dripping remnants, the remains of all flesh, their iron lengths tapering violently to the dullest point possible that still would pierce skin if with the most martyring of pain, points dappled with manifold shards of rust, strands of sinew, hunks of tendon smeared with yellowish and oily fat, spiraled serpentine in intricate nearly King Solomonaic ornaments of hair in many hues: a lightly spread carpet hovering just above the slumberous bed, a netting of heads' hair and toupees' and wigs' all meshing in a rumor of transparency, in the sheerest shades of black, lightest gold, gingy-red and gray to smoke's white floating just atop these nails pointing every which way as if in the shock of total accusation, the sting of absolute blame.

He stood at the lip of the Valley of Nails and said his Salaam then was quiet. We are all the saying of Allah in the voice of the man named Mohammed and so when I say my Salaam to the man named Mohammed I am saying it in His voice and It is Allah that is saying It, which is Him, which is It, through me, for me and as me as well. However I must say it, too. My mouth must submit. And so then he said his name on his own. And his address. His Aba's telephone number, his Queen's own maiden name and that of his Queen's mother, which had been Smilowitz, his Queen's Queen's, the half he remembered of the many digited identification number of the MERKAVA Mk. 4 V-12 diesel 48 round he remembered, as such was the tank that his Uncle Alex known as Sasha to everyone but him had half driven before he'd been fully desked through the streets

of Gaza at night and around its fences and then around and around them all over again, his tank itself a fence, a fence of one plank, in the morning merging into a fence of all tanks and again, Salaam Salaam Salaam Salaam and Salaam to all of which there was no answer but wind.

A stirring in the Valley of Nails, a living presence that then incredibly without disturbing the nails, their disposition and without, either, the warning of a rattle, the dull clink then clank of slimy chains — enormously a serpent slithers itself out of the Valley its entire foreverlong, nail-dark length scraped then sliced by the nails it lived in and among, rendering it a skin of scrape and slice always in a state of shred, always in many states of many many sheds no longer. The snake hisses me in, intimates I would say that it would guide me in and through, would lead me to the other lip of the Valley of Nails and so to the man named Mohammed who if not dwells then is shut up here and there only. I say Yes I say and as the serpent throws itself at me, as the snake lunges directly at me on its one good hind leg, upon its infinite, volutinous treelike trunk that seemed, as much and at the same time, the corkscrewily coiled pod of that carob wilted, almost totally exhausted as if it's a great effort to strangle me

in — I jump away, I turn around then run as if it's
not heaven but the weekend and I'm still in
sneakers not school shoes or those stolen and
naked now, turning again to face the snake
only at the distance of a lung, from atop a finger
of salt grown out from Heaven's face on which
I'm standing, panting, almost hurling myself
exhausted only to behold the serpent limply
fallen to the ground, its tongue hanging longingly out, pig-pink fading to an aspect royally
purple distended amid the darkness from the
lip of the Valley, forked in two directions different though equally nowhere, as dead as I stood.

BEit

I am of rabbis
a scholar to Torah and other
words, noted in my day
(which was long ago now)
and still in this day
by some who pray at
my grave because they
can't pray to me as I
am dead in this heaven where,
when soon after my
death a student of mine my
greatest student died and visited
me, found me on a beach-
chair on an approximation of the
beach with its ocean (Netanya)
alongside a film star or starlet I
never know which her name is, was Elizabeth
Taylor and though
she's dead to look at she looks pretty
good in a light whitish thong and blindingly
bleached sunglasses as my student,
my greatest student he approached, sat
down on a just-then-materializing beach-
chair and said:
Rav, Rabbi, it's so good to meet you again and
here, but I don't understand he said
throwing his tricolor beard and their chins in
the cardinal direction of Miss Taylor, Elizabeth

emerging from the wavelets, foam on her nipples and
all soaked to the bush but I don't understand he
said, how heaven could be like... this,
how this could be... heaven,
and so I said as I would always say as I stood
up in the shul in Witz but here I was at the
beach (Netanya) I said his name was Nathan,
Natan I said you must trust, but also think because it
might not be my heaven, I threw off my black
unshrouding the bronze of my chest,
it's her hell

LIMITATION

Limitation is what I now understand to be the sole attribute of God, at least the sole attribute of God or of A god we are able to apprehend, at least I am.

Allah says through the man named Mohammed through us, and so through me. For Allah to say To us is to render us dead from the dead.

If we were to experience anything above and beyond the limitation of God we would be destroyed above and beyond any afterlife's salvation or Savior. Above and beyond the succor of any appeal unheard. Above and beyond the Above beyond. And unspoken. No paradise can assuage the experience of the illimitability of God. Just as no Eden exists for those who know it as Eden.

As I am translating these thoughts from the air and from the wind of the air that speaks in no language, please excuse my attempts.

Atone, repent. Repent for atonement. (And atone for you know.) All like the instructions given upon a box of frozen foods my Aba often bought for dinner when the Queen was away visiting her sister in Arad. Like gel for the last Wash your hands. Rinse & repeat. As we say when we're live, don't adjust your TV.

Understand I am making these translations to atone. Understand I am making these translations repent for my failure. Understand and do not pity, sympathize or empathize, identify with nor enable, me. Who will translate:

To shove your gray tablets down into a moldy old sack wrought of skull, skin and hair, and especially after having held them aloft high above the dunes and the drops in pure, lifegiving sky, is not a pleasant duty but nonetheless duty. What Happened to Your Face? the Queen would always ask and what would I answer. Tongue-tied to the mullion of a window like the red rope of Rahab. What's That on Your Chin? the Queen would always ask, meaning my mouth, which once was unglassed and silent. But before I say anything, I want to say this: to my Aba, I've never smashed rock to make water flow flinty. No one's ever wrought a calf out of nothing.

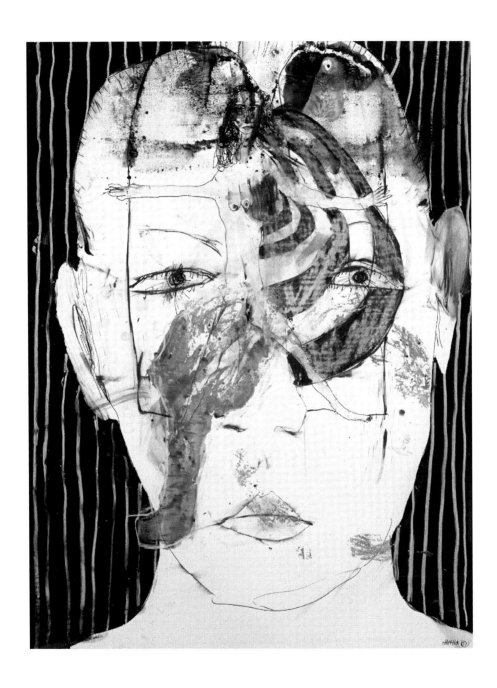

I never entered into the Valley of Nails not even as unshod as I was, and because I never entered into the Valley of Nails between the Two Mountains that might have been clouds after all I never had my Salaam answered, neither did I then truly seek the man named Mohammed and so neither did I then find any man by that name. Or by or with any name other. Truly. When it came to the ultimate sacrifice, I demurred. When pain entered into the world, my dream exited, flying. When a single choice was offered me I chose another. But a distinction must be made between limitation and weakness much like, in Hellenist heresy, the division obtaining between the light of the Gnostic Pleroma Aba liked that word in Greek And its warring dark and so might I then mention that I had and I believe still have and will always have a brother whose name was David and is. A half-brother actually if he ever was mentioned, he wasn't. He was fifteen, sixteen, seventeen or eighteen years older than I suppose he still is. And if so then seething. Why I didn't mention him before is that neither Aba nor the Queen mentioned him much or at all that I remember and that this gloss unlike forgetting was not unintentional. Inexcusably unreasoned as this David was the son of Aba's previous Queen, a woman who before I was born (of course, of course) had died of a dis-

ease that has afflicted many on earth and will
go on afflicting them as long as the earth is not
flat and is instead shaped like a Secular tumor:
"well-rounded," period-shaped, whole-note-
shaped, paint-blobuled in blue upon the neck
of Ibrahim's God — a disease afflicting though
only the living (though need I remind anyone
that there are less dead people on earth, or *in
the earth*, than there are people now living),
which begins gradually with the gradual
growth of a third breast, an epiphytic or rather
parasitic subspecies of maybe even sentient
mammæ and a harder type one, too, rather
Lumpy and lumpish and Bumpy and *bumpisch*
as Aba he once described it to me one Sunday
as we were out walking & talking in the Old
City having passed through the Jaffa Gate and
walking when talkatively straight as my Aba's
appetite for history and its revelation would
allow us to the Kotel, to the Westernmost, Wail-
ingmost, Wallingmost limitation of our need he
said it was A big black bumpishness that just
grew larger or rather filled you largely despite
what the doctors would empty, which despite
the nail of any needle would never be enough
to empty It all — Aba himself never went to
doctors, he went to the Queen, by which I mean
my first one and only his second — and so this
Queen, that former Queen whom I never knew
her neither her name even she was blackened

as if burned like a bush once consumed, turned Big Aba once said and full of blackness (Aba saying all this with a measure of ash and a shekel, one in each lung of his scales it then seemed), first the big black bobbing lump then three big black bosomy breasts budded up on her who She was very beautiful and once a very very famous concert pianist, too (according to the official photograph of her young in Romania Aba kept in the pantry locked with Göbbels, his gun), had three big black breasts that swelled to take over her entirety or rather the rest of her shriveled into, shrunk, was sucked into these three huge black boobing breasts that themselves then merged into this one single unified huge hard black breast, A protuber Aba who he was THE professional tuner once said he became such as he was because *she'd been* THE professional pianist: One enormous blob ball of cancer Aba said once it was he Had to sit with and pet — as if to bounce? — all night and with the dipped then wrung out washcloth he applied to its *roundingly dull shininess* though In the morning it had lost its roundness, by then it had further dulled off to become this hulking huge big black square As hard as rockstone Aba he was pacing Around and around and glancing at nervously as if it had just fallen through the ozone on down from space, Aba circling Aba

circumambulating seven times as she did for
their marriage vows, then the shattering of the
glasses of the seven subsequent nights of dinner then dancing in celebration of their
blessedness praying prayers my Aba didn't
know he knew as he was circling all this time
this monstrous circling and monstrously hulking huge big black square stone rock of death
that had crushed and collapsed the bed, their
marriage bed, which had been a gift from her
parents my Queen, Aba's second Queen she
later threw out to the Poor her piano It was just
sitting there in the room, Aba said foursquare
her taking up the whole room entire until Aba
he that afternoon said he just shut the door and
then locked it (as he had another piano to tune,
To take out of warp, had scheduled an ap-
pointment, always did or just always said so)
and returned that night the eve of Passover to
relieve the former Hadassah Medical Center
nurse who she was now named Hadassah, too,
and Russian as well as short and almost as bald
As a hardboiled egg at the Seder Aba had
hired out of the hospice, its rotation and then
asked her to stay On-call forever, until the very
end with its ice on the lips and the huddling
snuggle but found her the nurse gone when he
opened the door to THE ROOM, in their room
all there was in there was this K'aba black
stone taking up the whole entire room and en-

croaching, too, its death up against the wall of
the open doorway As if threatening to spill its
immaculate hardness all over the threshold and
then into the hall as Aba once said — upon
leaving the Kotel then returning home the way
we'd arrived, through the Old City through the
Jaffa Gate, toward Jaffa Road again and its walk
to Tchernichovsky Street and then down it —
he Just slammed the door hard shut then
locked it again and then went to pace around
and around and around nothing at all, to guard
over nil at the funeral home, ANTSCHEL'S FU-
NERAL HOME the sign said that we would pass
on the walk from Jerusalem to home if ever we
took the shortcut we never did.

David was not spoken about (and is obviously not spoken about anymore, in this way, by
this family), because at the age of eighteen,
which is the age of induction into military serv-
ice that for him would have most probably
meant Uncle Alex's Givati Brigade whose sym-
bolic mascot is the farting fox as plumed in a
purple beret, he forsook Jerusalem and the
Eden surrounding for a position in Hollywood
across the finger of sea and the hand of the
ocean — exchanging our trees for their open
palms — where he met and then lived with and
maybe still lives with a fellow Hollywood-trans-
plant, an aspiring Movieperson whose sex

meaning gender was less important to Aba
and even to the Queen (Aba's then-new-
Queen, my own) and still would be, if only, than
the religion — sexual — this Movieperson sub-
scribed to, subscribes. An affiliation this
Movieperson's name and his way of pronounc-
ing it Her apparently made quite clarion clear.
A lifestyle that David's severing of all phone
cords and unreturned postcards made even
clarion clearer though not the clarionest, which
was Aba's refusal to ever think or even know of
him again as his son and the Queen's full support of such a decision, which might have
made her love me even more, which was Nice.

But moviepeople and my half-brother are
not important As such. What is important is that
I, a son of my Aba's old age and the Queen's
hopeful youth, did not enter into the Valley of
Nails to save myself from the inexact succor of
this heaven, my hell. What David did and
maybe still does is David's, and it's my parent's
life to have thought that a weakness, a flaw. In
that standing at the lip of the Valley of Nails I
had a revelation. A revelation not swallowing of
the earth but my own. Whatever David did or
did not — and I never knew him before the
now in which I know all — whether a weakness
or no, was done, or undone, to others, too, no
matter intention. Which if not unforgivable has

passed unforgiven. I forget. That I have only myself to answer for. Now.

That I am alone here with no parents. And a stranger only insofar as I am thought strange.

His turning around and back from the lip of the Valley of Nails was not weakness. Neither was it limitation, however. As that might is not of me or ours. Rather what he did was give choice to choice, put question to question. What I did I did, and is done. Remember that the dead cannot sacrifice. *Never again!* And, too, that it is not for the living to judge the sacrifices they are bound to make, we all are — just as Cain and Abel and Aba's always saying of them in answer to my question as to why I didn't have natural brothers? as I'd always wanted one or more of them, any thousands of millions the Queen always said she'd been asking ever since I knew it was moot.

Listen, when one choice is a Jacob and when one — the other — choice is an Esau, I sought the brotherhood merited in, and gracing, surrender.

☞ Listen we can say limitation, too, when we say about the borders of heaven, the lines of demarcation, even of, yes, inevitable, attrition. To say heaven is borderless, without borders as if they were unnecessary, superfluminously superfluous, is to say the thing that is not. Or at least A thing that is not. Rather heaven only appears, is only sensed first dully and then, once accustomed, dimly perceived and then said to be — known and — understood, as borderless. In life. Indeed heaven must be understood as borderless if it is to have any borders at all, with its reflection holding as well: that because heaven does undoubtedly, indubitably, have borders, it must be first sensed only dully, then, once accustomed to speculation of such kind, dimly perceived then said to be understood — by those alive, on earth still, with no opportunity to truly know All — it must be understood or at least said To be understood by the living as limitless, illimitable, all-encompassing All, absolute, totally without end. (After all, it's only because the possible not to say probable human span is not eternity that humans such as I once was ever valued our lives.)

But let us drop our other weapons and ask: then where, exactly, are these borders? the endlands of heaven? what do these boundaries

consist of? when were they mapped out, de-
marcated, drawn in the sand? and who guards
them who guards the guards and all of what's
required to pass? questions the — an — answer
to which might be this: that Heaven is wherever
both bodily and of-the-mind the people of any
given heaven might dwell. *And how is the pop-
ulation decided? How is a particular demo-
graphic arrived at?* Outside this encampment,
In the beyond, there Heaven does not exist.
Through time, through dimensions and their
lands, a heaven's size, its volume, a heaven's
space, its mass and its density, its purchase and
purview is that of its inhabitants, its incarnates
or more faithfully to all its incarnators if you will
say It along with me. Wheresoever they might
roam and wander, so roams and wanders
Heaven. How and what they think and know
(*what they think they know*), so is the sum
thought and knowledge of Heaven. Why they,
so why Heaven. Who they, Heaven. As, Heaven.

☞   Indeed the walls of heaven, *which are walls*, quite physically, actually, appreciably, walls, move with the people, up and rearrange themselves, reposition, set incursions, Interfada hazarded against and within the Infidelis as We the people as the Americans always say set themselves toward realization, toward truest experience of heaven, and so wall in and wall out that that is made false, rendered untrue, anew each edging of the golden plate — or dish — serving up no sustenance at all. Insubstantial. In fact, under this quite contested, controversial, interpretation, the vast golden plate is not necessarily a dish of gold or a plate (which would explain say some newly arrived proponents of this interpretation why it serves up only nothing, or nothingness), rather it is an always moving, always wandering, always movable, always wanderable, hole in the wall that is the sky, a necessary hole allowing no escape into the light and its warmth that both says and means death from this heaven this hole in the wall of vaulted sky guards more securely than any quote truer unquote wall in its stead, any repair, any vaulting sky in its place, could ever hope to.

Because Mohammed says through me Who can sense walls in such darkness? That such a hole is necessary, a prerequisite, to our knowledge of the wall and as importantly of what it walls in and out. Up and down. I think of David sleeping, a wall suspended horizontally just a breath, newborn, above his sleeping form. And nearer, so near that when he awakes, when he opens his eyes, their lids become stuck in a crack, become wedged, in a crack badly mortared, mortally, between two huge, possibly loosening, stones. The wall halves his Hollywood room. No one lives above. It would be disrespectful to place feet upon his wall — a floor without anything atop, not even a rug, a shelf without a book, merely a rung left ladderless — one night, I know, the earth will quake and he'll breathe this wall in. Deepening sleep. Try to say an esophagus of breathed stone.

ALEF

On Rosh Hashanah, which
means the head
of the year in that language the
new year in Heaven, which
does not know from new
years we still try to observe it's
funny, our habits don't
die like we do

On Rosh Hashanah,
which means the head of
the year in that language in
Heaven you can ask for
God for one thing

On Rosh Hashanah,
which means the Head
of the Year in that language
in Heaven you can ask
God for one favor,
    one lack,
        won't insult Him by asking for
        that assuredly One thing only that
        might be missing,
that you might be missing,
even in a heaven that's yours —

People ask for

Everything on that Day of Days,

Ask for bad knees again, bad teeth, ask for

Car problems, erectile dysfunction, ask for

Everything except what they

need.

MATURING TO INFINITY

A boy grows. It's inevitable as is any Aba's pride, by which I mean heartache — the two of them panned, weighed in honest enough scales slung across the gray dead of his eyes. A boy grows because he must. To know the earth from further. Height marked short above the threshold, at seven, eight years a full two hinges tall. A screw stripped to posture. Turn the knob. A boy matures. Even in Heaven. Even in the wrong heaven, which, in the endless end, is more a question of Who. Behold the Who becoming another Who who by the time he's become yet another Who is by then wholly unknowable. Me. Open the door. An eternal boy matures eternally. What do you want to be when you grow up? the Queen always asked though she had all the answers, as if breasts to suck to satisfaction, hers as much as mine. A nipple doctor? A slip 'n' fall lawyer? Wait. Maybe a government minister? Perhaps an Israeli? A Semite? I know — a Jew?

No not a doctor and no not a lawyer and no not a government minister — not even with nor without a portfolio. And Yes, who wants to be a Jew when they're grown?

Maturing to infinity is not the worst of all means. Neither is it the worst of all ends. It is a becoming unnoticed and unnoticing. Nonetheless a becoming. A becoming still. To mature is not to grow up but to grow In, is another dimension of growth I was never to have realized had I survived, had I lived. No one ever does in life, I mean realize, recognize, Actualize is what the Americans say except of course for the Cabbalists and the — good — Slavic poets and that ancient I think she was a woman in that tablecloth stained then knotted around her head into a kerchief the Queen she gave a shekel to outside the Kotel because her as Aba said Birdosaurus pecker of a face seemed to prick her and hard. But no not even them I say, that the realization of true growth occurs only in heaven, that only in heaven can this growth begin only to never end ever. That in heaven one grows eternally and infinitely In. Through yourself. Into your skin.

In heaven maturation is unending. Maturation is ripening not to rot but to riper. To grow unendingly is the ideal, with an aspiration to tempered by a recognizance of the impossibly ripest: a sheen of skin under which our lives are packed deep, tightly, juice straining the thin peel of neck, exploding the seeds of our Adam's apples to sow a wind for the gleaning of our inconsolable widows. Upon the Messiah, we will become arisen as if worms to our fruit, to live within and without the world simultaneously, surfacing for air, then again burrowing down to the core. Bite us in half and we will grow back ever bigger. Call us a snake and our tongues will no longer be bitten. Understand. This is what we once believed. I am sorry. This was once the belief that was us. We beat our breasts at which we have suckled our gods and our murderers. Forgive us. Forget nothing.

Yea though I walk around this heaven unshod a boy, in appearance to all those who would not know me to be me a snot-faced, pit-fisted, brat-child of ten fat years of lean age, the mind within — or lo the soul, if that you prefer — has or was gifted all knowledge at death, all knowledge of all of the All (along the way losing any sense of personal, or let's even say tribal, achievement), and, further, was given the opportunity, perhaps burdened or curse-laden with the opportunity to know itself, to know within, in depths denied to the living. To the floorless ocean floor of all mind from whence we arose to beach ourselves back when. Maturation to infinity means evolution, though not of the kind they taught at the school on Tchernichovsky Street the Queen, for one, didn't want me to know about but which Aba he never seemed much to mind: Galápagolgatha & co., all that business with the ape-monkeys, them mating abominably with their cousins the chimprillas, all of them hooting themselves into pillowy moustaches, argyle, paisley-hatched, widow-sheaved, fleurs-de-lis socks limp like intricately patterned foreskins distended from their Tush-wiping, opposable paws, underarmpit-sniffing themselves into most auspicious important bank and clerical positions, nits and grubs being rendered vital to the matrix of State, a centrifugal integration of instinct as opposed to the six nightless days of Creation and only then, the prime eternal seventh of rest — Shabbos, when the true effort actually began.

To say again because repetition. Because repetition is the death of death.

To say maturation to infinity means an evolution beyond who you were born to be. Means a boiling to the point of air. Means an assimilation to the sky and its vault. Never forget the vault. To say an escape from all conditions and contingencies inescapable in life. A means of divestment, of all assets to prove anything but. A denial of inheritance. Dissent from who. A negation of lines, fences, walls in the shade of their very existence. Exigencies. Means that though I am in the wrong heaven it is only because I think this is the wrong heaven (and so to say that once I believed the wrong heaven was possible, that wrongheaveness was in fact fungible, a presence the universe does not contradict nor even challenge). Doubtless I will mature past all thought at some future of eternity. Now. Or other. Soon in the oases' prism of soon, I await. An I, I wait doubtless.

Listen and I will say what I have said. In this heaven as in any heaven I am no longer a Jew. In this heaven as in any heaven I am no more a Jew than I'm not. Jewful and Jewless. Listen. Then hear. Understand. To be religious in heaven is to be truly fanatic. Every day is no day and is Sabbath. There is no more reward. There is nothing to live for and no whys to pray. Listen in no heaven am I named what I once thought my name was. What once I Jonathan knew my name to be. What my Jonathan had been according to those who had named me (Aba and the Queen, after my greatgrandAba dead) and not what my name is of myself. My name for myself is now merely Listen, to follow

the laws, which are merely the hatreds, of the
living while in heaven is to disrespect your own
death. To adapt. No longer. To survive. Not anymore. In no heaven is my Aba my Aba, and the
Queens here are no Queen of mine. To be forever estranged, even amid your own congre-
gation, and to be forever wandering, even
within your own encampment, and only because they make me a stranger, and only because they make me a wanderer, they who
would be I only if, I who would be they only
why — the self-elected elect, the self-chosen
chosen, the self-righteously rightful inhabitants
of this heaven who are still religious, amazingly
so, even here, who have here become even
more religious, ever more religiously religious,
amazingly so, especially here. Listen to my
mouth disembodied. Hear through my ears,
one pierced, the other is shredded. Understand through me exploded, dispersed, en-
sharded, in pieces. That parts of me: a finger, a
toe, a nose or else a liver, an antique residue of
our anatomy: a spleen — they are still occasionally what those alive would regard as sen-
timental. Nostalgic. But this, too, will pass.
Sometimes the death of these habits or tradi-
tions or laws (whatever you want to call them,
they're called) saddens me in the extreme.
Other times the passing of these frequencies,
these inevitabilities, these inescapables,

makes me happier than the vault can contain. Mostly however I am ambivalent about and to this death. Thriving off the fund of numb. And so to my death, too. Sunned. Both were inevitable. Are. Or at least one happened and another will happen, and so you will notice that I still say and so think Will happen because a mind of mine still needs to think of or at least wants to believe in a future. Listen that that, too, will pass. Into waiting for waiting. Which will pass as well, on its own. There is no waiting in the future and there is no future in the (you understand). Listen and then passing will pass. Hearing, too. Again await the all over again. Understand, then listen anew.

A part of me: usually the head of my penis, or my left sagging testicle, the enraged animal yellowing a kidney of mine or else a fetus forever gestating there, maybe the taboo hindquarter of either thigh, perhaps my right fluttery eyelid — all destroyed once, all to be made whole once again and again in the sanctuary of every memory had — a part of me, whichever part, now still holds fast, cleaves one can say in my first language: Cleave, which in American means both To rend and To adhere, To cling close or Cleave that Aba said often Cleave that Aba always said was one of his favorite words in any language, in any of their opposing definitions sundering two meanings from one sound. Whichever shard of me cleaves to, still cleaves to and must cleave to history overwhelming. Whole half a millennium of waiting and waiting for redemption when our true redemption was in the waiting. And waiting. Again scales, slung across the whites of my Aba's dead eyes again. If only he could have seen me now. And especially now that he can't. An allowance, allow me. I left my permit in my pants on my body in blood on the earth. This me an indulgence as harmless as the Three popsicles? how the Queen always said You indulge him too much and how Aba would-n't disagree before dinner, bathtime, bed and then sleep (the way those red pops would melt from their ice to water is my stain on the street, sticky with litter and pain). And so while this me lasts, however longingly long, I should like to consecrate this homesick history, mine — to vial and stop this mad gushing past. To save it. At least a portion thereof. To store it up for the famine attendant on hope. Bottle it corked for the Friday. Not for the sake of martyrs or teardrop lineages, of victories and all that insensate fell star stuff who could ever have hoped to have understood in life. But for and only for the sake of Them, theirs a sake of one dark's duration it seems to me now if only for Their sake. I and this is almost too difficult, too said for me to say that *I cleave* to this identity for and only for the memory — mine — of my Aba and the Queen. For them how I loved them. And for the expectations they once had for my own memory. Expectations becoming love in their ripening. A memory to be had by others. Becoming. Others I never made in an image I felt becoming the world.

A "METAPHOR"

Alef-Beit-Alef. Heaven is like the early evening or as Aba always said Dusk into evening into night late night into early morning or as Aba always said Dawn of my tenth birthday the night before the day I died the morning I was murdered exploded incendiaried bombed blown up blasted away anyway I died (but I didn't know that then I only knew that the Queen wanted me needed me to go to sleep but first to have my bath and made Aba make sure of that though only after our dinner beginning with mushroom soup during which Aba said that his Aba my grandAba had known all the different kinds and multitudinously multinuminous species and other taxonomical types of mushrooms that he had picked them for years From the forests around his house in It wasn't then ha'Ukraine Aba said It's called mycology the study of mushrooms this Mushroomologic that there must be something to it this Mushroomtry this Mushroomsophy he went on and on laughing to himself until the

Queen said to Be quiet and eat your soup it's
getting cold The Soup Aba always ate with a tablespoon and I always ate with a teaspoon
though it was soup and not tea with mint which
would be served later though sometimes To
demonstrate solidarity with my son as Aba always said he too ate his soup and not just
mushroom soup but also pea soup and at other
times beet soup which is called borscht and
tomato soup too occasionally with a teaspoon
and not the tablespoon Aba usually used
though he never even once ate a table with it
and which the Queen always used to eat her
mushroom soup too which was set alongside a
fork with which to eat her salad with Three firm
ripe tomatoes the Queen always said and three
peeled cucumbers and one pepper green with
envy of its seeds removed to the trash as the
Queen always said A few small green onions
say three of them For good measure then olive
oil good olive oil and the juice of half a lemon
and salt and spices *Hyssopus* Aba always said
and sometimes even When I'm feeling adven-
turous as the Queen would always say when
she'd added ginger grated or else a few chilies
or at other times maybe a very small pinch of
pepper Cayenne then mixed them all up together and they're called a salad these ag-
glomerates of different vegetables liquids and
spices this amalgamation of diverse produce

sprinklings and oil is called by just the one word *Salat* the most important word to the Queen this Salad prayer the Queen always said to Eat your salad to grow up strong and live forever with your health As if a wife and so we did my Aba and I ate our salad and then the fish which fish I didn't know because while it's easy relatively easy to say that this is a chicken and that this is a cow that this is a lamb and that this is a turkey it's difficult Relatively difficult as Aba always said that even meat it was Einsteinian or arguable at least for me to differentiate among and even between fish or fishes like the two Dags I had had one I flushed the other I hope's still swimming around and around the Kinneret which is the lake to be found under the sea up in the Galilee I've thought about how it's relatively difficult to distinguish which fish is which fish we had with a dill and lemon juice and paprika and mayonnaise homemade mayonnaise sauce to dip then for dessert a platter of fruits dates figs apricots and pears dried and fresh and nuts that was a present for my Aba from An elderly admirer all the way out in Gilo whose piano the previous week he my Aba had tuned for free then cleared the table to leave the dishes Don't forget the pots and the pans too to the Queen so that Aba he could give me my bath in the water he first had to negotiate with always first

had to negotiate with negotiations were always
going on in my house our apartment because
our water was strange or rather it was that the
process necessary to obtaining a temperature
of the water or waters appropriate to desired
for any given purpose say bathing me was A
process as strange and as involved as that of
any political negotiations Aba always said what
exactly it was was that the hot water tap pro-
duced only the most hot water gave forth the
height of hot water and that oppositely the cold
water tap gave forth only the coldest of cold
waters almost freezing though not scientifically
freezing as Aba once explained was 0° Anders
Celsius of Uppsala and so to achieve a livable
median an acceptable if muddied middle-
ground of water temperature for conducive to
let's say bathing me required An artful and ex-
perienced manipulation of both taps and so
both temperatures the boiling and the freezing
to A happy medium Aba always said the two
taps those twinned faucets pouring individually because it was An old porcelain tooth
bathtub Aba always said it had to be replaced
soon enough Any day now the Queen always
said and so the mingling and so the mating of
the two waters As if husband and wife was ac-
complished not down at the Dead Sea Desalin-
ization Plant or in the Jerusalem Reservoir then
through a unified pipe up through the length of

a solitary faucet but in the tub and on me and around me and over me splashing in the tub having my bath with all my splish toys the boats and the buoys and the frogs those many rubberized squeezies that I would leap enormously as if they were ADD/ADHD lambs mated with the most unmedicated of rams from the wilting lilies of the gunky green faucets to crash the cruising ships and tankers to bob the buoys transmitting their blip bleeping signals of distress gurgling as the soap would always become drowned in the whirlpool lost between my thighs just as my Aba would want To wash my punim Aba always said then to wash my hair and rinse the stinging yellow green snot from out of my nostrils and my hair which he said resembled a certain bush Moses once talked to in the wilderness of Sinai the wide purple towel the Royally purple one the Queen's extra which I always got to use when she didn't need it when its Purpler twin wasn't in the wash and there smelling of her and even feeling of her skin that softness it was Aba's as he pinched at me still dripping now running from his pinches and dripping still soapy water to darken the Oriental rug actually Persian Sultanabad and infinitely ornamented with various flora that as dead didn't require my watering of them in the hallway atop which my Aba chased me then cornered me against the

wall of the hallway under the photographs of
relatives dead themselves as only imaged in
wood and in glass then picked me up upside
down to walk more like stagger with me hanging my dripping head down between his legs
that walked all the way to my room banging my
wet head then one of his bad knees usually always his weakest one that he hurt once in East
Jerusalem and once again in Eilat on the door
to my room and saying a word I know but I'm
not allowed to repeat as he my Aba began with
the story he always told me about the Rabbi of
Polyn or with the stories he always now told me
about the Rabbi of Polyn or else the one he always told me too about an eagle or sometimes
a hawk or a raptor or maybe even a raven at
other times that flew down when Aba was out
on incursion excursion or exercises up in
Lebanon that flew down and stole off his helmet which got him into serious trouble Another
story he said it flew with it off and away because Birds Aba once said are the first to disrespect national sovereignty because birds are
always the first to disregard territorial borders
flew with Aba's helmet straight to Jerusalem
and there to Tchernichovsky Street our building and its third floor to the Queen's kitchen
window which was always open because as
Aba would always say We should always keep
everything open Aba always said Our windows

our doors our minds & our hearts and the
Queen who took it of course Aba said as a sign
that Aba was dead either killed by the enemy
or else in quote friendly unquote fire how he
was hostaged or missing in action until Aba
came home a week later because Aba he always came home and found Aba said that the
Queen had not only just found out she was
Pregnant with me he said but had also just
used his helmet as a bowl in which to mix up
the batter of a cake in some versions an apple
cake in others a plum or plain bundt of any
cake she was then making for the old women
woman Or maybe it was a man Aba said Aba
didn't remember and often told it either way
who then lived downstairs in what would later
be the Maier's apartment but who now was
dead and is still who Died a day before or else
After your bris Aba would alternately say after
the first mohel he didn't show up with the
guests waiting around like pent livestock then
the second mohel the first mohel's son didn't
show up either by the time they'd already
gorged themselves on all of the rugelach all
ten trays of the stuff I'd had to order in from
Marzipan down on Aggripas Street Only the
best meaning only the most costly for the
Queen as she wasn't just then in any shape to
slave in the kitchen for all these guests drunk
with the schnapps and the wodka I'd laid out

and some even felt it necessary to leave early
and others to go to sleep to take a nap on the
couch by the time the third mohel he showed
up the son of the second mohel and the grand-
son of the first his grandAba who finally did it
and did it well though he and despite his having been brought up as a Kotzker a Gerer anyway insisted on sucking away in surprise Aba
said I was nervous it being the third mohel's
first bris yours I mean being the first er um
putz the Rav ever cut though all turned out fine
better for you than for me I mean what with the
amount of drinking I did even after it all was
over and you were back to bed sleeping
soundly Aba said as you should be sleeping
right now it's so late and so instead tonight that
night I mean to say he my Aba told me no story
at all not the Polisher Rebbe story and not the
story of Lebanon Aba said it was after all Alto-
gether too late and said further that if I was
good and went to sleep right away meaning
not much later than now then he would owe me
not one but amazingly two stories for tomorrow
night it seemed we had begun bargaining hag-
gling handling like this was the Shuk as if this
were a table I had had in a past life in the
square at Peshischa and not my very own bedroom in which Aba would be beholden to me
for both the story set in Poland and the
Lebanon story and so I said to him Aba Okay

which is an American word we liked to say to
one another I said 10 – 4 B.ravo C.harlie Fine
by the movies agreed to his terms You're the
boss I said which we liked to say too because
what else could I do besides what I then did
which was to try to get to sleep right away because now at least then it felt like I had something to think about something or other I
should think about to remember if just to pre-
serve it like pickled pomegranate or like the
jellies the preserves and the spreads that
downstairs Misses Soloff used to make from the
fruit flecked with the rusty rind of the etrog
both sour and sweetened them the many versions of these manifold stories and all in my
head as I remembered them or tried to remember them then To compare and contrast
them as my teacher Moreh Kulp at the school
terribly next door on Tchernichovsky Street always said to hold them both up as if the two
tablets of the Ten Commandments to smash
against Aba's fivefold versions on the night that
would begin not tomorrow but the day after
that would after all never dawn but when Aba
he said the Shema O Israel the Adonai our Elo-
haynu the Adonai is One both Adonai and Elo-
haynu and many other names just as much I
didn't then know as he kissed me goodnight
Laila Tov as he turned out the light I found
much to my astonishment dismay mystification

perplexity too all of them and at once I could-
n't just then remember any version of either of
the two stories he my Aba most often told
whether it be the Poland story or the Lebanon
story or even the occasional Time the Taxi got
me Lost in Queens and I Missed your Cousins'
Wedding story I couldn't then remember either of any of them that night and not even my
favorite or favorites which was the Polisher
Rebbe story which were or could have been on
any one occasion any one of three Polisher
Rebbe stories none of which I could then remember that night that in one of them the Polisher Rebbe was asked by a Prominent Gentile
though it's not known as the Prominent Gentile
Story "Do gentiles have souls?" and the Polisher Rebbe answered him "that since you a
gentile and a Prominent Gentile at that asked
that question that that question must then stand
as your proof and as ours that Yes you indeed
do have a soul" while in another a man he's a
Jewish man and he's dying an Old Poor Jewish
Man he's dying as usual and the Polisher
Rebbe he tells him to go to the Polisher Priest
and convert to have himself converted to
Christianity Catholicism whatever it is that they
believe in the Popes and so the poor old Jewish
man goes to the Polishist Priest and converts
and lives In fact he lives only because he converts but when the next New Year comes

around Rosh Hashanah meaning the Head of
the Year how he heads to shul anyway his feet
take him there and for the very first time since
his conversion it's as if he felt he had to go was
impelled felt compelled by Something the God
of the Other and that the moment he crosses
over the threshold of the shul the synagogue it
then falls in on itself collapses and crushes all
the assembled and praying to death their own
Kaddish in the third Polisher Rebbe story the
Polisher Rebbe receives prophecy in a dream
though in another occasional variant a highly
placed and paid Police Informant informs the
Polisher Rebbe that gevalt a pogrom is to take
place tonight and so Der Polisher Rebbe that
was his name he goes to all of the town's the village's the shtetl's tailors and from them collects
tailors' dummies all of their mannequins and
then has them all dressed up like Jews then
sends for all the Jews' goats and cows and
calves and chickens too for all of their animals
and has them too all dressed up like Jews Aba
said Like Hasidim they looked with their dark
hats and dark suits and white shirts and dark
yarmulkes and white tzitzit and black payos
and cool Asian imitation RAYBAN sunglasses
on all these tailors' dummies for the gentiles
Goyim to slaughter instead then evacuates all
the Jews all the Real Jews to another town a
nearby village a neighboring shtetl though just

for the night during which they won't sleep a
fortieth of a wink like me because when they
all return to their shtetl the next morning early
at the rise of the sun they find a whole ghetto of
Jews they'd never known before whom they'd
never seen before in their lives never heard of
Jews all cleaning up from last night's chaos dis-
aster and mess sweeping up window glass fa-
thers mothers mopping and children all the old
tailors' dummies and livestock brought to life
come to life conscience and good housekeep-
ing and so the Jews have to leave there's no
room for them anymore in their old houses An-
cestral homes Aba said they have to abandon
in search of another homeland to find yet another Source Aba said are the stories that night
I forgot the stories I couldn't recall I couldn't
remember that night though I tried and I tried
no matter how hard squinting my eyes then
pressed and then pushed on my stomach like I
do when I'm trying to go to the toilet To pish
before bed which I forgot Aba always insisted
upon but just as standing At military attention
at then sitting upon the Waterless old newspaper older magazine toilet that night lying I then
couldn't and soon enough I tired myself out
with just thinking or actually with not thinking
about it at least trying not to think and instead
I occupied myself at least tried to with reading
all of the titles off all of the books high up on

the bookshelf or shelves all the way across my
huge it seemed then room it seemed in the
dark facing my bed as if to swallow me with
their many mouths which were only shelves of
more teeth which were books but I could only
make out then I could only read the titles of the
books that were closest to the crack of the door
the sliver of hallway's glowworm nightlight I insisted on remaining open and on and those
books they just had the same titles I knew from
every night I remembered A HANDBOOK OF
SOCCER RULES a few fake abridged versions
for kids of the selected works of Jules Verne
HOW TO SPEAK GERMAN IN TEN EASY LES-
SONS and then as a bookend a Tanach with my
bar-mitzvah portion bookmarked with a leaf
from the "aspen" in our backyard I had to
begin studying in the fall the same portion my
Aba had the first one which is the portion
called Genesis of the book that's also called
Genesis because *In the beginning* I had a late
summer birthday like my Aba with the
Haftorah from Isaiah *Fear not for I am with thee*
I will bring thy seed from the east and gather
thee from the west I will say to the north Give up
and to the south Keep not back bring my sons
from afar and my daughters from the ends of the
earth the same titles I knew from each night I
did this which was almost every and still I don't
know why I didn't just go ahead and up and re-

arrange all the books on my shelves why I did-
n't just put new titles there then move some old
ones around others but I never did ever and so
quickly it seemed but it probably wasn't I was
bored of the titles and so then moved I wan-
dered my eyes to the left or so to stare dead
ahead then at the crack of the draft at the door
at the seam the scar of the suicide attempt of
the wall its light that was coming through shining though getting narrower and narrower or
rather becoming shorter and shorter smaller
too it seemed as if a rectangle becoming a
square becoming a yellow circle that was like
a block I used to play with that the Queen gave
away to my new cousin in Arad I hadn't yet met
and would never becoming a generic cereal O
I would string as if to bead a bracelet or necklace on a shed of the Queen's hair drowned in
my milk whole in the morning becoming just a
pinpoint a prick the sting of a wasp's afternoon
one for both of my eyes and yet one for each
too imprinting itself singeing themselves *in-
cising* and *gashing* until despite the pain I fell
asleep finally I must have fallen asleep then at
long last I fell asleep I did as dead as I am now
and will be forever and there yes here yes this
was what I am after this is what I've been after
what I was trying to say what I'm saying that
heaven is like: when I fell asleep and into a
dream but into a dream THE Dream that might

or might not be new novel or original but I'm
sorry it was a dream at least I'd never had before and certainly not since I dreamed of
dreaming and that was it was a dream of a
dream only in which I was in bed with the cov-
ers with the Aeroplanes on them the helicop-
ters' propellers and rotors tangled up to my
nose with my eyes closed and that this is what
I saw what I thought what then happened was
that I was sleeping and that I knew I was
dreaming that I was dreaming of sleeping and
in that sleep I was dreaming that was it that was
all I was forced was compelled it's that I was
cursed to dream myself dreaming and with
everything around me the same and unchang-
ing and me unable to change it or myself I was
straightened into this dream of dream into this
dream of a dream of a dream with as many lev-
els or hierarchies or heavens' worth of con-
sciousnesses if you want attendant upon the
phenomenon as I can now attempt to admit
then to know understand that was it was without revelation there was no revelation there
was none at all to be had and instead though
it's a poor bargain if you'd ask me now only if
you could only if I could answer in return the
assurance of existence that's it times tenfold
that that's all that I am shining I'm just shining
through the horror just through the raw yolk of
existence cracking a shine through its knob-

less handleless shell it was horror yes because it Was horror or rather more accurately more faithfully it was terror yes more like terror that was it was terror it was abject terror abject total terror yes terror that's what heaven is like that absolute truly terrible dreaming of dreaming of mine.

Yom Hazikaron, 2004

By Joshua Cohen
The Quorum
Cadenza for the Schneidermann Violin Concerto
Aleph-Bet: An Alphabet for the Perplexed (with Michael Hafftka)

Joshua Cohen was born in southern New Jersey, in 1980. He is a writer for *The Forward,* and lives in Brooklyn, NY.

By Michael Hafftka
Michael Hafftka - Selected Drawings, 1982
Art of Experience - Experience Of Art, 1981
Conscious/Unconscious, 2007

Hafftka has had one-person shows in New York City since 1982 with Art Galaxy, Rosa Esman Gallery, DiLaurenti Gallery, Mary Ryan Gallery and Aberbach Fine Art. His work has been shown in the US and abroad in numerous museums. Hafftka's work is in the permanent collections of major museums including The Metropolitan Museum of Art, MOMA NY, The National Gallery, Brooklyn Museum, San Francisco MOMA, The Carnegie Museum of Art.

Hafftka's work has been the subject of critical monographs by Sam Hunter, Professor Emeritus of Art History at Princeton University, John Caldwell, Curator at the Carnegie Institute Museum of Art and the San Francisco Museum of Modern Art, and the novelist Michael Brodsky. Hafftka's work can be seen online at www.hafftka.com.

colophon

Epigrams are from Nelly Sachs, *Glühende Rätsel (Glowing Enigmas): III*, and Saul Tchernichovsky, *Levivot (An Idyll)*.

Titles: Kowboy by Adam Hayes and Nick Hayes
Text: Rockwell by Monotype Typography
Cover & book design: Michael & Yonat Hafftka
Cover Art: Michael Hafftka
Proofreading: Christine Webb

Starcherone Books is a signatory to the Book Industry Treatise on Responsible Paper Use, the goal of which is to increase use of postcon umer recycled fiber froma 5% average at present to a 30% average by 2011. It is estimated that attainment of this goal would conserve 524 million pounds of greenhouse gases yearly, equivalent to keeping 45,818 cars off the road, as well as saving the equivalent of 4.9 million trees, 2.1 billion gallons of water, and 264 million pounds of solid waste each year. We thank BookMobile Printing for making this option available to us.